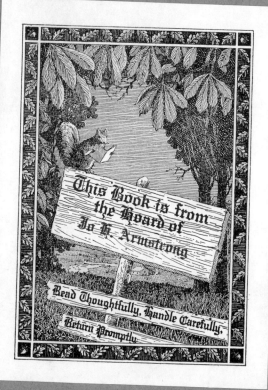

This Book is from
the Hoard of
Jo H. Armstrong

Read Thoughtfully, Handle Carefully,
Return Promptly

# THE SALT OF THE EARTH

# THE SALT OF

# THE EARTH by CARLO MONTEROSSO

Translated by Isabel Quigly

PRENTICE-HALL, INC., ENGLEWOOD CLIFFS, NEW JERSEY

The Salt of the Earth
by Carlo Monterosso

© 1965 by Carlo Monterosso

Published in Italy by Rizzoli Editore

First American Edition published by
Prentice-Hall, Inc., 1967

Library of Congress Catalog Card Number: 67–22021

Printed in the United States of America

T   79100

## CONTENTS

Part One
The Testimony of John,
called The Baptist

Part Two
The Testimony of Judas,
called Iscariot

Part Three
The Testimony of Thomas,
called Didymus

*Let us regard Him and His life, let us speak about this quite humanly, for He was very human indeed.*

—Kierkegaard

# THE SALT OF THE EARTH

# PART ONE

The
Testimony
of
John
called
the
Baptist

THE TESTIMONY OF JOHN, CALLED THE BAPTIST. I am setting down my evidence on the eve of my execution at the will of Herod and the instigation of Jesus, the traitor. I remember the day we first met.

How beautiful he was, how gentle, how smiling and pure! And how clear his eyes were when I looked up from the water where I was washing my clothes, and saw him approaching. I did not speak, but waited for him to present himself.

"Master," he began. And how sweet, how perfect his voice seemed.

Still I did not speak, though I realized a smile was slowly opening up in my beard. He went down on one knee, but I withdrew my hand, and made him rise. I had seen the color of his eyes, deep blue, like velvet, but without a touch of vulgarity. His hair, that gleamed darkly, hung in tidy curls.

"I have come to see you, Master."

"Have we met?"

"Yes," he replied with that ineffable sweetness of his that had already poured into and possessed me. "Because I have always wanted to meet you, Master. I am from Nazareth in Galilee. My name is Joshua, but they call me Jesus."

I picked up the clothes and wrung them out, and avoided looking at him, knowing why I did so. I wanted to repeat the pleasure of seeing him. Pleasure is what I call it, but I mean excitement; something that was not pleasure, but a state of mind I had never known before, halfway between fear and joy. I felt small. Just then, I was afraid one of my disciples should see me. I looked up.

"Why have you come?"

Jesus noticed my harsh, awkward tone, and smiled even more openly and submissively.

"To be baptized."

That feeling of trepidation, of joy, of being suddenly saved from the total solitude I was heading for, turned into obvious fear. Oh, how right I was to fear him from the start! I should have listened to that first unconfessed re-action of mine and rejected him. Instead, in one of those outbursts that men of faith put down to the infallibility of their impulses, I seized him by the shoulders, bent him over into the water, immersed him.

Was I sincere in wanting to keep him down longer than necessary?

I was, and now I know that my fear was so strong that I should have liked to kill him. Instead I made him rise, and embraced him excitedly.

"Jesus," I said ecstatically, gazing at his brow, "I baptize you in the name of our Father who is in heaven."

At that moment a smooth stone shifted, swept along by the current of the river, which ran swiftly a few yards from us. I saw a gull watching me from the riverbed. He spread his white wings and flew over us, very close, then moved away. I felt I must become practical and busy.

"I'm glad you've come. You'll help me a bit. Go and get wood, we'll light the fire and have something to eat."

"But I shouldn't like . . ." he murmured, smiling.

"I like you," I said, looking at him, and the smile brought us together. I saw him walking diligently towards the hill, and could not help watching him. Even in his movements, in the way he was searching, he was grace incarnate. He did not exist. All the time he kept revealing himself.

"I see you've got a bag!" I cried gaily, as I was spreading the clothes out on the large smooth stones. "You wouldn't have salt, would you?"

"Yes. And boiled eggs!"

"Any fresh figs?" I added, growing ever gayer. We sat

down near the clear water and ate with enjoyment, talking, revealing ourselves to each other, becoming more and more friendly. I feel nostalgic thinking back on it. How I loved him, right away!

❋   ❋   ❋

He was only a year younger than I, but the gap between us seemed at least ten years. He was ageless. When he spoke he showed a wisdom that seemed to come from endless ages. I, the Master, listened to him fascinated, even if he said things that were in no way new. But as he spoke they were new, perhaps because of the way he put them.

He stayed. And when my disciples, who had gone into the nearby town for the weekly supplies, came back to the river, they could scarcely believe it. Had I allowed a man I had baptized to stay with me? In Elifaz I noticed a little jealousy. Natan took it calmly, though.

We spent the Paschal feast on the Jordan, immensely busy. At least a thousand people, men and women, came to be baptized and Jesus stood aside from it. The fact was, he always stood aside. Let Elifaz and Natan, both of Sichar, confirm what I say. When he spoke, he was withdrawn from us. When he was silent, his presence was like a light from above. We felt he did not belong to us.

He had special ways of behaving. Like eating delicately, even in poverty.

"You don't exactly stint yourself," I reproached him good-naturedly one day.

"No," he replied, with the smile that disarmed me. I watched him. He was clearly a soul determined to perfect himself. The vigor with which he held the arms of a man being baptized showed how he was determined to act in the spirit of the rules. Everything he did was sanctified by faith, you could see. At least, so it seemed.

I surprised him watching me as I was meditating. I had retired to the loop in the river where the whirling water grows crystal clear, circling, like pleasant thoughts. Kneeling beside the stony bank I was staring into the water, my mind at rest. But that evening, a stone broke the enchantment. I turned.

Jesus was above me, on the dune.

"You?" I said, bewildered.

Another stone fell into the water. His hand was still shaking. He came down to me, and sat back on his heels to rest.

"I've watched you more than once, Master. What are you doing?"

Puzzled and disturbed, I replied:

"Meditation and prayer."

"Wouldn't it be better to pray together?"

"Prayer," I replied, "is solitude. We're not people who need to go to the Temple."

"And is that the whole difference between you and the others?"

I considered before answering: "Yes, that's it."

"Then you won't go far," he said, rising. He was looking beyond the river.

"Do you mean you're leaving us?" I asked him, appalled.

He was already leaving. "Yes. Because men are saved by going among them."

"Don't go!" I shouted, following him. He seemed the Master. Elifaz, at the camp, stopped to watch us. "You still haven't understood the reason for my preaching!"

He faced me squarely and for the first time I thought him hard.

"I've realized you're a vegetarian with a good digestion. You baptize for fun. Would you suffer if you had to?"

"Don't I suffer already?" I cried, hurt, and unexpectedly racked by doubt. "I live on nothing and only I know how nature's solitude and indifference weigh on me, some days. What do you think, that I'm a fool?"

He dominated me. And as he walked away without answering, I called after him, stricken: "But what do you think? What is it?"

I heard he had gone back to Nazareth, stopping two days at Jerusalem. Zacchary, who came from Bethany to see me, said he had seen Jesus in the Temple wandering among the merchants' stalls, and that he would try and talk to, say, a group of priests, or a troop of Roman legionaries off duty. He followed him and saw him settle down in front of a dice-player's table, lay a bet, win, and walk off with a girl.

But he had not left me to go in another direction. After a month he was back. Three companions came with him, and that same girl, who cooked his food separately from the rest, made his bed and cleaned for him. The three men stood round him, their muscular arms crossed.

"Magdalen," he ordered her. "Go and offer a chalice of wine to the Master."

The girl came up to me holding the jug. "Lord, why do you hurt me in this way?" I wondered. Elifaz and Natan, mild and impotent, stood behind me.

€18

"Drink," Jesus urged me, sitting on his stool.

Or else he would come himself and, with a change of tactics, look at me again with that infinite sweetness that had overwhelmed me. Even if I tried I could not raise a hand to say: be off.

"Master," he would begin with infinite sweetness, "speak to me of God."

And I, subdued, would say a psalm of David's.

"The assembly of the wicked have enclosed me: they pierced my hands and my feet. They part my garments among them, and cast lots upon my vesture. But be not thou far from me, O Lord; O my strength, haste thee to help me."

Tears ran down Jesus' cheeks.

"Are you true?" I said, leaning toward him in a torment of expectancy. "Are you the revelation?"

His eyes closed, his tears dried, he looked long at me, his indefinable smile absent, indifferent. They stayed three months and I heard that two of those three ruffians had been brigands on the road to Jericho. I saw them lay their spoils at Jesus' feet.

*　　*　　*

People now came to me in crowds and I still cannot explain why. It seemed natural, the ripening, then the picking of the fruit. I had not noticed my popularity. Perhaps some new repressive Roman law, or a growing despair at the thought of never being free, sent people thronging to be baptized in the Jordan. One thing alone I knew—that this crowd was calmly inspired by God. There was no religious hysteria, there were no mystical outbursts, but men and women coming to purify themselves from their sins, trusting in, if not yet expecting, a better world.

I was weary, worried, and embarrassed. I wondered if this unexpected success was what I had wanted. My object had been to spread the word "Repent," but now I selfishly regretted the days of quiet meditation, of improvement through sobriety. They brought me presents, even money. Elifaz and Natan had to take on assistants to give the poor what we had so much of. But some of it, inevitably, stayed with us. And so, in the evening, there would no longer be the grasses, salted and ready for me, but delicious food that tempted me. And since there was nothing else to eat, and I was in a hurry, I ate it.

"Master!" they would say, their arms raised, offering me things. "Our family cloth, dyed with purple we have made ourselves!"

Or else:

"We bring you the savings of generations, that you may intercede for us!" And at my feet they poured out baskets of coins that glittered in the water.

Riches that surely looked forward to some power in the future were heaped up on what had been a dull bare patch of ground by the river. The gull had vanished. The water had turned muddy.

Yet what could I do but accept, and try to organize?

It was during this time of abundance that Jesus reappeared. He was wearing a white garment, which his girl, still the same one, bent down to raise so it wouldn't get dirty. His henchmen I failed to notice: later I found they had mingled with the crowd.

As it was a feast day, the riverbank was crowded. Many people were bathing. The ground was strewn with scraps of food.

"You?" I stammered, turning pale.

He knelt down and kissed my hand, and either because he looked so gentle, or because the girl had knelt too, people near us were silent and moved away.

That would have been the moment for me to shout: "This man is Satan!" and at my words the crowd would have drowned him in the river. Instead I withdrew to the edge of the circle, leaving Jesus in the center, irresistibly appealing.

"Who is he?" I heard people murmur. The women's faces were enraptured, the men's, curious.

"We are fortunate to be allowed to drink at the Master's fountain," Jesus exclaimed.

He was already walking across to the water, and knelt down and drank. As corn spreads across the field in a wave when the wind blows, so the whole crowd bent over. They sipped rapturously from the palms of their hands. The pallor of Jesus overwhelmed them.

I had stood still, while Elifaz and Natan came up behind me. Natan, always the gentler of them, was the one who spoke out clearly: "What has he come for? Shouldn't we throw him out?"

Elifaz observed:

"I've a feeling there are others with him."

"Who told you?"

I looked around too and noticed that in the shadow of two tents where they were selling wine and lemonade, a dozen youngsters were lolling about, some on stools, some on the ground, on the meager, dry grass. I hurried over to them.

"Who are you? What are you doing on my land?"

No one answered. I looked at the oldest, who was in the

center and might have been older than Jesus. He raised his cup to toast me.

"It's hot," he replied, and indicated the pleasant shade.

"Who are you?" I shouted.

"Peter," the man answered indolently, like a man refusing to be ruffled. And he pointed carelessly to the others: "Andrew, James, John, Philip, Bartholomew, Thomas, Matthew, another James, Thaddeus, Simon, Judas."

They stayed all the next day, when many who had been baptized left, and then half the gang vanished, leaving Jesus with the other six. He occupied the largest tent, on his own. The girl lived in the one next to his, and the others were crowded into the third. They were oddly silent; at night there was not a sound.

On the fourth day, when it was completely dark, I saw a pale figure.

"Well?" I heard Jesus' voice, gentle but brisk. He was alone, and obviously waiting for me. I went towards the river, meaning him to follow me, though I did not realize it. The water, lapping timidly, told us when we had reached the bank.

"We've got to talk and know where we stand," Jesus began. "First of all, what's your object?"

Ingenuously I answered: "God."

"Yes, that's fine. But on this earth?"

My heart was hurting me, because I felt that what I had always dreaded was happening: I was in for a statement of accounts, and had to admit I was not up to the situation. I was not suited for action.

"I've never meant to have an object on this earth," I answered uncertainly. Then, realizing my mistake,

I added hastily: "I mean an organized object, giving my faith a system."

"But you've got an impressive following," Jesus said slyly, "and you can't keep it without an organization. I mean, you're all set to establish a party."

"A party?" I tried to avoid this tactless suggestion. "But there are so many parties already. The best party means being on your own."

"I know being on your own's the most comfortable," I heard him say sarcastically. "But you can't be on your own any longer, because I'm here. What's to be done together? The time's ideal. Tension's growing against the Romans, and with all these followers we shan't lack funds. You've seen how they're ready to give. As far as getting the word around, I've set up contacts in several towns. Six of my men are busy in Galilee just now. The easiest way would be to start there. What do you say?"

"Why in Galilee?" I asked, though I knew that what I should be doing was refusing, not asking questions.

"Because I know everyone there and I'm known. The rich are just waiting and they've promised me practically limitless funds already."

"The rich?" I said, bewildered, incredulous.

He seemed to hesitate a moment, and if it had been daylight I could have read his eyes.

"They want order," he replied. "They've had enough of riots and arrests of people refusing to pay taxes to the Romans, smashing up their insignia, making ambushes. Enough of all that. Order, order, order."

The vision of a country pacified in God, that had overcome all it suffered under the occupation, glowed before me, and at that moment night turned to day. I thought I could see the river flowing calmly, the water playing clearly between the banks, the distant hills in bloom. Smoke rose from the roofs of the houses and doves lazed on the tumbledown towers. On this wholesome if hackneyed scene, even the sun seemed to shine contentedly. I sat down on the riverbank. No more would I need to baptize, because the people were now purified and already lived in the Kingdom of God, which was none other than the kingdom of man in peace.

"Yes," I murmured, as if to myself, "we've had enough. And if it goes on like this, there'll be worse to come."

"Mopping up pockets of resistance, curfews, burnings, deportations," Jesus sat down and spoke softly. "The coast barred, Jerusalem blockaded, the Temple destroyed."

"Oh that," I exclaimed, "would be the least of our evils!"

He was silent, feeling with me. Then he began to speak, and a shudder seized me:

"Blessed are the poor in spirit: for theirs is the Kingdom of Heaven. Blessed are they that mourn: for they shall be comforted. Blessed are the meek: for they shall inherit the earth. Blessed are they that hunger and thirst after righteousness: for they shall be filled."

Yes, yes, I prayed within me.

"John, you mustn't think I mean to abolish the law; I don't suggest abolishing it, but completing it. Don't you think the only solution is to bow our heads to the oppressor? Don't you think being realistic means accepting that suffering is unavoidable, and, by this acceptance, overcoming it?"

"Why didn't you come to me sooner?" I asked, enraptured, and now, as I reinvoke him, I love him as I did then.

He continued, in the starry night:

"Because I tell you this, that if our justice isn't greater than that of the Temple, we shall not enter into the Kingdom of God. It has been said: 'An eye for an eye, a tooth for a tooth' but I mean to tell our followers: Don't resist evil; on the contrary, if someone strikes you on the right cheek, turn the other to him. If someone fights to get your tunic, give him your cloak as well."

He lowered his voice and added, altering his tone:

"Of course the two of us know the oppressor in question is the Roman soldier, but we shan't tell our followers—that would give the game away."

"The game?" I turned to look at him. He stayed quite still, as if he had said something he had not meant to say, yet. And this was how he revealed himself:

"Yes, the game," he repeated decisively. "Game in a good sense. For the people."

"But you were talking about the rich . . ."

"Of course. They're the ones who will give us the means to get organized. Money. But above all, storm troopers. Armed, I mean."

"But didn't you say we should repudiate violence?"

"Against the Romans. But among ourselves, to bring order among ourselves, we can't do without it. Don't you see? Only among ourselves."

But that was where I began not to see. He realized this, and so tried other arguments: that the landowners needed order more than anything, so that they could carry on running their affairs in the interest of peace; that the Tetrarch wanted exactly the same thing; that it was all the people themselves wanted as well, only they didn't know they wanted it; that in this way our party would be trusted by the whole country, it would be the national party and the pair of us would lead it, with the Romans' approval.

"The party, the party!" I exclaimed, trying to control myself. "I can't stand all this talk of a party! Our people's never been a party, it's always been the people of God."

"Exactly," Jesus agreed, with satisfaction. "So we'll ignore the Romans and concentrate exclusively on God. But wasn't I perfectly clear? I'm not proposing to abolish the law, but to complete it. Can't you see quite clearly how we've evolved, historically? Our laws have given us ideas that are incomplete and often contradictory; they've got to be examined and arranged. They must be made into a coherent whole to renew the country. We'll recall people to the fateful Mount Sinai, to the greatness of Moses, to others God chose in the old days. We'll draw the people after us. The landowners already like my ideas. Which are yours, too, aren't they?"

I thought it over, dismayed.

"Yes, but in a different way. Some things I can't quite see. Will the landowners turn the other cheek to the Romans? Will they hand over their cloaks?"

I looked at him with love: "Your own sublime words!"

Jesus laughed, leaning slightly on my shoulder.

"But they won't need to! No Roman would ever slap a landowner, still less try and run off with his cloak! Oh John, won't you really understand?"

An immense light suddenly put out, the sun melting away without even a feeble spark left: this was what I felt.

In the darkness of that spiritual death, I felt my look was on the face of Jesus, feeling it was slimy.

I put out an arm, sideways, to push him off. At that moment the gull, that had been absent for months, flew over my head. With tears in my eyes I followed its flight in the darkness, as it grew huge and white, like a bellying sail.

"Very well." I heard him rise and arrange his clothes, which glowed dully. "But you must think it over. You're not alone any longer, you know. I am here. And I have greater means than you."

❊  ❊  ❊

The crowd of those who came to be baptized continued to grow. They came in caravans and I had to make them take turns. I would line them up, and Elifaz and Natan would let them come forward one by one. I no longer even immersed them, but just sprinkled them, and then they immersed themselves. Often Elifaz had to remove the hysterical; occasionally a woman would fling her arms around my neck. I no longer liked it: it was obvious we needed an organization.

Indeed, since it was all a threat to public order, a squad of Romans with a warrant officer in charge turned up. A delegate from the Temple came with them. The warrant officer asked me for my license to trade, and I explained that it was not a business matter, that people did not come to pay me or to be paid, that it was a kind of entertainment.

The squareheaded Roman looked around wearily.

"But it can't go on like this," he said.

I replied that it depended not on me, but on him. If he

wanted the crowd to leave, he should send the guards of Herod, who was in charge of this territory. I knew this would not be easily done, because ours was not an entertainment, but something more, as Herod realized. Indeed, the warrant officer said:

"This is an unauthorized political meeting."

It was at this point that Jesus appeared. He had come up to my tent without my noticing.

"May I come in," he said, coming forward, and I saw the warrant officer's face altering, like that of a man awakening. "Only God can authorize a place of prayer. Give Caesar what is Caesar's, and God what is God's."

The warrant officer looked at him.

"Exactly," he said. "Caesar commands this meeting to disperse."

"But God doesn't." Jesus stood up straight before him, sweet and proud. "And this is God's meeting."

The warrant officer consulted with the Temple delegate and they moved off towards the wineshop tent. Jesus told me softly:

"We must stand firm and show them that God is our only inspiration."

"He is!" I wanted to thunder, after so many bitter days. He made a movement to hold me back.

"We know, we know. But the Romans are in command. Can we go on like this? Look at this mob along the river, hanging about much longer than it has to. I've already found cases of stealing and violence. Don't you feel the need to clean them up, to give them a system, an organization? Wasn't that exactly what Moses did in the desert? Don't you want to give them a party? Give them a religion!"

I was kneeling on the ground, with my head in my hands.

"I feel that everything's on the point of being lost," I groaned.

The warrant officer came back, and told me that for the moment he would take no action, but that they would watch the scene for a few days and then decide. It was obvious that the Temple delegate was behind this: the man himself could hardly follow it all.

That night, when I was behind a thicket, I heard footsteps. I stopped. Voices were speaking softly and I immediately recognized the voice of Jesus, then that of the Roman warrant officer. By chance they came and sat on the large stone by the waterside, just in front of me. It was a sultry night, the sirocco was blowing in slowly from the sea, bearing the smell of orange groves, and the moon filtered uncertainly through the low clouds. Nature was dull.

"Have I made myself clear, centurion?" Jesus was saying, addressing him as centurion though he was nothing like it. "Nobody here wants to disturb public order, still less to rebel against you. They're people dedicated to God, superstitious people who think they must take orders only from above, as in Moses' day."

"Who?" said the warrant officer.

Jesus took no notice and went on: "So direct orders might be dangerous and provoke resistance. What you need is a man you trust who'll be able to keep this mob in order and make it do what you Romans want."

"But what about this fellow who baptizes, wouldn't he do?" said the Roman. "He's the boss, isn't he?"

I heard Jesus snigger and reply:

"Yes, but he's not the right type. He's a mystic, and refuses all action. Do you know what a mystic is? But we could persuade him to let us use his name. Here!" And I heard him passing something over to drink, then a smacking of dry lips.

"This is what you must say in your report," Jesus continued. "You must say these gatherings aren't dangerous but might become so if they're not organized. If you like, I can come along and explain this."

The Roman answered something I could not hear, and they both moved off towards the tents. I followed them and saw what I was expecting. Jesus put his head into the girl's tent, the girl came out and joined the warrant officer, while Jesus retired.

Three days later the Roman squad left. The Temple delegate came up to me, smiled contemptuously, and without a word followed it. As I expected, Jesus disappeared the same day. A week later a small troop of camels, men on foot, and dogs turned up.

Natan said:

"Rich folks. What have they come for?"

They were, in fact, landowners.

"Who is John who is called the Baptist?" one of them shouted without dismounting. Elifaz went up and soon afterwards the man dismounted, and the other four or five did the same. There must have been about a score of them altogether, masters and servants. But only the one who had spoken came up to me, the others immediately went over to the wineshop tent. He wiped the sweat from his forehead, ran a cloth under his armpits, sniffed it.

"We wish to speak," he said, without even looking me

in the face, while he took off his shoes and slackened his belt. He nudged a servant and told him to spread out a rug; then at last he looked at me. The other landowners, having quenched their thirst, were coming back. They sat down in a semicircle in front of me. The servants had quickly put up a tent and were fanning the warm air.

"What do you want to know?"

"What we want to know," the man replied, looking straight at me as merchants do when they are trading, "is what this business of 'repent for the Kingdom of God is at hand' means. What is it, now?"

As briefly and dispassionately as possible, like a lawyer, I explained it to them.

"Right," said the man, sniffing at the cloth and flinging it away. "Now what we want to know is this: in order to await the Kingdom of God, do you really have to annoy the Romans?"

"We don't mean to annoy anyone," I replied.

"But the fact remains you do!"

"You do, you do!" echoed the other four or five.

In honeyed tones, their chief went on: "Now, here's what we propose. You persuade this crowd, which is getting rather large, to respect the Romans, pay their taxes, stop cursing them as oppressors and instead consider them protectors; in short give up their dreams of independence, since they never will be independent—and when you get down to it independence isn't that exciting. What counts is good health, work, food, drink and enjoyment."

"Independence only means trouble," said one of the others.

"Yes, nothing but trouble," said another.

They echoed one another like fools, and I felt like telling them we were not aspiring to be independent of the Romans, but independent of sin. But suddenly I remembered what Jesus had suggested, and then I understood. In dismay I turned. He was standing behind me.

"And in exchange for what you do for us," the man continued, but I was no longer listening, "we'll give you a kingdom on this earth. Is that clear?"

Still Jesus did not speak, but I felt him growing enormously behind me. He moved and went over to the semicircle of landowners, standing enigmatically behind them and smiling faintly as he looked at me. The landowners' spokesman meantime kept pressing the need to give the country order. Herod himself had spoken to him about it, and seemed determined to intrude in some unpleasant way, starting with me. If the people wanted peace, they must make it themselves, and the first step was not to irritate the occupation troops.

"But the way to do this is something we must discover for ourselves—which means people like us: myself, you, him, the rest of us. The ordinary people are too ignorant."

I gave no answer.

"Well?" the man asked.

"The Master asks for time to reply," said Jesus.

He leaned down to the ear of the landowner, who agreed reluctantly, and the group rose stiffly. The servants had put up some double tents, red in color, and they all went across to them, their legs aching from the long camel ride.

At sunset Jesus appeared before me. He was on edge and spoke dryly.

€32

"It's clear now, isn't it?"

I murmured to myself: "It's obscure."

He made a movement of impatience and went on, in the tone of a man who means to waste no more time: "Agree, or it'll be the worst for you. These men haven't come here just to talk. They want to settle things."

"What things?" I was on edge myself.

"I explained it all to you. All you've got to do is say yes."

"And why not say no?"

"Because you've got no choice."

I got up and towered over him, and at the same time, just because I saw him defenseless beneath me, I felt an immense tenderness for him. There was a lump in my throat as I spoke:

"I know you're not sold to the Devil. It's the Devil that's got into you and possesses you."

He turned his back on me, clenching his fists.

"Go away into the desert and meditate," I told him, clasping him to me like a father. "Come back to me purified, and together we'll pacify the country in God."

He turned to me, blazing:

"Listen," he said, changing expression with the speed that always tormented me, "I can't throw away this chance. If they don't have me, the landowners will choose another man they trust and you'll be in the same position you're in now. Don't you want to act? Agree to come along with us. I'll speak to the crowd. I'll persuade them in your name."

How long I stayed on my knees that night I do not know. I must have slept in that position, because I was awakened, still kneeling, by the first drops of rain. They fell heavily on the dust and the first flash of lightning lit up the glassy, hostile river. In the thunder that followed I felt I heard the voice of God commanding me. I went to my tent.

"Master?" I heard a whisper, after a while.

"Elifaz? Natan?" I asked.

Two shadows appeared, then others. Before I could speak they had prostrated themselves and were waiting at my feet. They were Zealots.

"You here?" I said, alarmed. I wanted no part of their armed resistance movement.

"We respect and admire you," said the same voice, reverently.

"What do you want?"

"To advise you, and, if you like, to help you."

"I don't need you, as you ought to know. Though in my turn I respect you too."

"It's impossible for us to avoid collaborating with each other," the man said. "Do you know the state of the country?"

"I repeat, I'm not interested in politics," I said, keeping my voice down. "I'm a man of God."

Very slowly they had risen and were crouching before me; in a flash of lightning I saw the handle of a knife.

"You're mad to come here. There are Romans about."

"They're everywhere," a voice said gaily.

"The country'll soon be betrayed," the first speaker went on, dramatically. "The landowners are in league with Herod, and Herod's in league with the Romans. They want to castrate the people with pacifist ideas and keep them down for good. You're the umpire in this whole business."

Once more I felt uneasy at having reached the day of reckoning, and sighed for the days of solitude and uninterrupted talk with God.

"I know," I had to admit. "But what do you want from me?"

"Just what you say. Go on preaching to the people the way you've always done."

"And who told you I meant to change?"

There was a short silence, then the voice said: "You don't, but other people want you to."

I was suffocating in that oppressive heat. "Who?" I asked.

"Jesus."

"Let me have some air," I said, waving my arms like a dying man. They opened the tent and in the lightning flash that moment I saw six faces, staring, thin, imploring, decisive. They were hardly more than adolescents. I felt I wanted to take them all in my arms and, sobbing with tears, confusion, energy, certainty and despair, I flung them off.

"We'll get rid of him," said the young leader, standing up to me.

"No, no!" I begged him.

"The traitor."

I fell on my knees, appalled at the prospect of Jesus hanging on a tree or actually crucified by the Zealots as a sneer at the Romans.

" 'My God, my God,' " I prayed, " 'why hast thou forsaken me?' "

35

" 'Many bulls have compassed me'," their voices went on for me, " 'Strong bulls of Bashan have beset me round. They gaped upon me with their mouths, as a ravening and a roaring lion.' "

I pushed them out of the tent, touching their shoulders, loving them. One behind the other they slipped out into the pouring rain. The landowners never came to discuss things with me again; taking advantage of the coolness after the storm, they left the next day.

"I've persuaded them the situation isn't yet ripe," Jesus told me quickly. "They'll wait."

He went away too, with the girl, but left that fellow Peter and the other five to occupy the tents. People kept coming to be baptized, and I baptized them, but without enthusiasm. I could feel life diminishing within me, as if I no longer hoped for anything in others. I longed to confide in someone, and it occurred to me that I might visit the Essenes towards Qumran. But then I thought this would be interpreted as an alliance, and that the Essenes themselves, keeping strictly away from politics, would disapprove of it. So I sent Natan to my old friend Raffaele in the community, asking him to come and see me at night; and he came.

We recalled the time I had been one of the Essenes, before retiring into solitude, and half-joking I said: "Without meaning to I've ended up making a community myself."

Raffaele told me the Essenes disapproved of what I was doing, that my preaching was subversive, and that I not only stirred up the people, thus laying them open to the Romans' oppressive measures, but drew away from God myself.

"We, on the other hand," Raffaele went on, and I was surprised to find him so pedantic, "stick to the principle of noninterference. To us, the daily ablution remains the symbol of life. The bath water removes all our vain aspirations."

"Hot or cold?" I said, with friendly irony. But my onetime comrade failed to understand. He continued preaching what I already knew and had repudiated as insufficient: physical cleanliness, traditional virtues, communism of goods, serenity, and, as the Romans brought up in the school of Epicurus put it, *mens sana in corpore sano*. I realized I could not confide in someone with a view like his, and watched him leave, taking care not to soil his white garment. In the pale moonlight I saw him make wide detours in order to avoid the puddles, jumping, and once protesting out loud.

❊　❊　❊

Days of relative calm went by. The crowd had momentarily diminished, although the throng on Sundays was enough to show me my own popularity. I baptized and, when there were not many present, I preached; always feeling I must repeat the same concept of repentance and that, even if I was bored, it was my duty. Many souls seeking light first found its rays in this.

Those who never came near me were the six Jesus had left behind. So one evening I went over to them. They were sitting about in their usual way, some perched up on stools, some on the yellowed grass. One was picking his teeth with a toothpick, but when he realized I was going to speak he stopped. But I said nothing. The man called Peter was the one who spoke.

"A chalice?"

I refused politely with a gesture, and asked, faintly teasing: "Aren't you bored yet?"

Peter shook his head, smiling good-naturedly, like a child.

"But what are you doing, exactly?" I went on.

"We're waiting," said Peter, without moving from his restful position.

They did no work, never went away, did absolutely nothing except attend to themselves, moderately, silently.

"And in case of need," Peter went on, "we're here."

The new might was there before me, men organized, silent, steadfast: doers. Technicians of power.

"But who are you? What are you doing here? What are you waiting for?"

Peter answered: "We're waiting."

"What do you do for a living? Why are you here?"

He changed his position and answered calmly:

"You never know. People might come and make trouble. Bandits, tramps."

"Soldiers as well?"

He smiled kindly, as if talking to a child: "Soldiers won't come and make trouble."

I thought I had understood. I withdrew. Indeed the very next day Jesus returned, with the girl and the other six, and came to my tent with all twelve, leaving them to wait outside. I found him rather tired, but in a hurry. He said he had come to decide and that he had the land-owners, Herod and the Romans on his side.

"It's nothing to do with me," I said dully.

"That doesn't matter. From now on you'll be in charge

here but you won't baptize anymore and you won't speak to the people. You've delegated your powers to me and you'll stay on and watch."

Lord, I prayed, why don't you give me the strength to oppose him? I wanted to say my favorite psalm, but lacked the strength even for this.

The words "My God, my God, why hast thou forsaken me?" rang tonelessly in my head, as in an empty gourd.

Jesus must have guessed my state of mind because he sat down, and his face lit up with a tired smile, as it hadn't for a long time. But he corrected this at once, and frowned.

"What I'm doing is necessary and inevitable. For the country. I'm sure you'll support me. Just now you may feel vexed or even indignant, but it won't be long before you realize I've got the right solution."

I managed to compose my voice enough to say:

"I'll never accept orders that don't come from God."

"God, God!" he exclaimed without warning. "*I* am God!"

I put out a hand to push him away. He realized he had gone too far and lowered his voice:

"This fixation with God. All our people have been doing for two thousand years is talk about God and believe they're God's people. But that's all over. Less God and more action. David didn't kneel around waiting for God to speak. He acted."

"He lived in God," I sighed in a kind of agony.

"Yes, but after he'd acted! Moses acted first and then said he'd had orders from God. This God legend! This fixation! We're God! Me, you, all of us!"

Blazing, he stopped speaking, and suffered. Next day

was Sunday and Jesus at once put his plan into action. From dawn onwards the twelve sat by my tent, behind which Elifaz and Natan crouched like a pair of good, useless dogs. As I watched them I remembered what Jesus had said the previous evening: that action was what mattered. And for a moment I was tempted to agree with him.

The crowd that spring day was enormous, and dappled the yellow riverbanks. I saw Jesus murmur an order to Peter, and he sent six of his men about twenty yards from my tent to prevent the people being baptized from approaching me.

"What a crowd!" Jesus said, with satisfaction. Then he added, with a little scorn: "Too many."

Later he went up on one of the dunes and began to speak. He repeated the concepts I knew, and the crowd gathered round him. Other unimportant speakers scattered on other dunes were left without an audience.

"Among men born of women," he said enthusiastically, "no one has ever been as great as John the Baptist!"

He pointed to me, stuck on my stool like a sick man, and the crowd swayed, breaking into a murmur of agreement. He explained that God had called me into a new cycle of meditation, from which I would return with new divine revelations. These, Jesus declared, would be the following:

"Love your neighbor as yourself, which is more than the Scriptures say. You know that it used to be said 'Love your neighbor and hate your enemy.' But John the Baptist will return from his meditations with this new revelation of God: 'Love your enemies, pray for those that persecute you, that you may be children of your Father who is in heaven.' "

So ineffable was the truth of those words, which were new to me, or at least seemed new as they had never done before, that I felt choked; and still as I was, I heard a hundred thousand hearts beating as their bodies strained upwards. Resplendent in the sun's slanting rays, Jesus seemed transfigured, and when he came down from the dune the people made way for him and followed him.

I envied that moment.

"Did you see how they listened?" he said excitedly to me. But he read my face, was embarrassed and added: "You mustn't take it as a personal affront. You know we'll both be running the party. Didn't you hear the way I praised you? It's still you the people want."

To get on the right side of me he asked my advice.

"I'm not sure whether to put this teaching, which would be a kind of prayer, into my talks. Listen: 'Our Father who art in heaven, hallowed be thy name.' Good so far. But then: 'Thy kingdom come, thy will be done on earth as it is in heaven.' That's what I'm not too sure about, because in the name of tradition they might conclude God's will is for us to free ourselves of the oppressor, that is, the Romans. Which would mean just the opposite of what we want."

I looked at him as a prisoner in chains looks at his torturer, without knowing whether he is real or an angel sent by God to tempt him.

"I don't want any misunderstandings," Jesus went on. "The landowners and Herod wouldn't forgive me. So I thought of adding: 'Give us this day our daily bread, and forgive us our trespasses, as we forgive them that trespass against us.' And at the end, quite clearly, this: 'And lead us not into temptation, but deliver us from evil.' That is, lead us not into violence, even against the Romans. Is that clear enough?"

I answered, but my voice did not come from me: "It is clear."

That whole night I wept and next day Elifaz and Natan found me so prostrate that they were alarmed. Their anxiety irritated me for a moment and I snapped:

"Do something, instead of standing about like sheep!"

Seeing them ashamed and imploring made me regret it at once. I realized their gentleness was exactly what Jesus was preaching and had secretly conquered me. And was I now rebuking them? I held out my hands to them, they came to me and the three of us stayed together, praying to the Lord.

But then, thinking it over coolly, I realized it was my duty to oppose what Jesus said, which was true but directed toward evil. I decided to speak to the faithful who had been baptized, like Zaccharius, Timothy, Jonathan, Naab, and Elon, and who came to see me occasionally. I was now waiting for the right moment to rise and start preaching again.

❋    ❋    ❋

But what followed was so unlike what I had intended and expected that I still cannot believe it. But dawn is coming, the iron door will be flung wide and the executioner will stretch out his hands. I must hurry. The new words flashed around the whole country and encouraged by the fine weather, people came as pilgrims to see me.

When they were sent to Jesus instead of me they were at first baffled, but quickly accepted him, and were as attracted as ever by the cool water of the river. To avoid coming into contact with all these people, Jesus had a boat tied and kept steady by a rope between the two banks, and from this he preached. Now and then he would come and relieve his feelings to me:

"What a rabble! Have you seen the way they try and touch me, the minute I get off the boat. They plunge in to be baptized and then try to climb up on board."

He now lived in a fine white tent that Magdalen kept immaculate for him. Everything inside it was also white, the carpet, the bed, the furniture. He had chosen the color of innocence, but it was hardly the color of poverty. His own white robe was changed every day and two other women had been brought to help Magdalen. He ate food cooked exclusively for him, drank fine wines brought especially for him, and had a shower built in the shelter of some branches. Round his small camp, which included tents for the twelve and one for the women, a fence made of pointed stakes was put up, and some of his men stood on guard there.

It was not long before other tents went up, also surrounded by a threatening fence, and I saw sinister faces peering over it. Lances and truncheons appeared.

"What's all this?" I asked Jesus.

"Public order," he said, laconically. Suddenly he looked at me, annoyed: "You don't do a thing and don't notice the number of people around!"

Some days he was nervous, because he was tired. He worked too hard, yet the way he kept on at his theme of gentleness, forgiveness, and giving up violence, never palled. His preaching was always gentle, seducing his hearers without their realizing it. Even I, who had learned his tactics to the last detail, was always won over in the end.

He had something I lacked. But what was it, brilliance or cunning? Was he an adventurer, or was I a fool?

In my heart I cared nothing about the answers to these questions. God manifests himself to men in various ways and what matters is that he does so. God might have manifested himself to Jesus through his sublime words, I felt, if only they had been sincere. But what I wonder is this: since they were not sincere, are they worthless? Might God not manifest himself even through a man who was flawed? Again I pray, imploringly: "Jesus, my soul, my saviour, why have you betrayed me?"

At the Paschal feast Herod's troops had to appear, in order to keep the peace. But hidden behind a hill two companies of Roman soldiers were waiting. In the glade, once so solitary, the loutish followers of Jesus, armed with truncheons, kept moving among the people, authoritatively clearing the way.

He, now absolute leader, seemed unchangeable. Though tired, he had a kind word for everyone, and he kept away the louts who rushed to protect him. He spoke charmingly: "Let the children come to me," he said.

He liked to appear at table with the twelve, right beside the river. The crowd would watch him ecstatically as he ate and he made it clear that he enjoyed eating, and appreciated the good things of life, to make people realize that good living would come only with peace and submission to the Romans.

A woman broke through the cordon and flung herself at

his feet, kissing them, bathing them with tears. I saw the face of Jesus contract with disgust, but then I saw it open into the sweetest smile as he helped the woman up.

He raised a jar of wine and passed around brimming chalices. Everyone accepted, and he continued to pour out the wine. He had climbed up onto a table and seemed to be trying to slake the whole world's thirst. Sickened, I left.

He noticed because I saw his expression change and when he came to my tent he did not hide his anger. He forced me to come back outside on a litter, and, having sent the bearers into the river till the water was up to their chests, he told them to raise me up high. The crowd roared its joy. I felt like a puppet.

That Paschal feast marked the end of my endurance. If I had had any doubts till then, they vanished. I sent for those who were loyal to me and told them what was happening. I waited.

"We knew it!" Zaccharius spoke first. "And we'd lost faith in you completely for not fighting back. But now we know God hasn't abandoned you. Command us, and we'll obey."

I loathed the very thought of commanding. What I suggested was that for the present we should oppose him quite legally. In other words, I would just start baptizing again and preaching in my old simple way. They all agreed. I now know that they agreed to their own con-demnation.

My first demonstration took place a few days later. While Jesus was baptizing I entered the water too, a hundred yards away, and, having raised my hands to heaven, in my usual way, I said nothing. Astounded to see me again, the people gradually came over to me. I cried:

" 'The voice of one crying in the wilderness, Prepare ye the way of the Lord!' "

Jesus himself was obliged to come over to me, and looked at me, surrounded by his followers. Kneeling down, he proclaimed with a voice so inspired that everyone there turned towards him:

"I must abase myself, that he may be exalted!"

A long, ecstatic song rose on the spring air, and even Herod's soldiers, camped some way off, rose and joined the crowd. At that moment I felt I had achieved the unity we had longed for of my people in God.

But that evening, when all was silent, and only a cricket fluttered the moonlit silence, the figure of Jesus appeared before my tent.

"You've gone mad," he said, his hand squeezing my arm like a claw.

With my newfound strength I replied: "God has made me mad and I obey his orders."

"Listen," he said sitting on my stool, bending his face over mine till he nearly touched it. "I'm directly in command of Herod's soldiers, which you see about the camp, and besides them, I've got my own storm troopers. I've only to raise my hand for the Romans to intervene as well. I'm not arguing about ideology anymore. I order you to stay in your tent during the daytime, without a break. You can come out only at night."

"I'm sorry for you," I replied, drawing my face back uneasily, "because you're walking towards the cross."

He leaned further over me, forcing me to bend backwards.

"After you, then."

"You're betraying your own people, and man, and God. So the Romans will betray you as well."

He grabbed my chest: "I'm ordering you."

I was choking. He left me. And next day I was still baptizing, and the days after too, and the crowd thronged round me again, drawn by my sincerity, as if it had regained consciousness and had realized it had been the victim of an illusion. It had abandoned Jesus. Then they swooped on us like hawks.

I had never seen such a sight. Truncheons raised, they spared neither the old nor the children. Clearly they had orders not to touch me, but perhaps for this very reason they were even harsher to the others. Bleeding faces, wild eyes, children limp in their mothers' arms seethed around me, looking for a way out that did not exist. In my astonishment I thought of the massacre ordered by Moses in the desert of his own brothers who had worshipped the golden calf. And then neither the shouts and anger of the oppressors nor the innocent faces in contrast with those of the armed ruffians managed to persuade me that this action, however cruel, was totally unjustified.

Was I a golden calf myself? And if so, wasn't Jesus justified in his cruel, scornful attitude towards those who worshipped me? One of the numb, wounded faces looked reproachful, watching me there unable to do anything, and seemed to be accusing me fiercely and openly at last. So it was I who was guilty!

I saw a knot of sunburnt muscles lashing down on a mother's head, and did nothing; I saw it whirling, heard the crunch of blows, and made no move. A child rolled over at my feet and an old man, hit in the stomach, stuck out a slavering tongue, as if in insult.

They were staggering about the ground now, like sand-bags punched in a gym. It had become a deaf, dumb, wearily methodical massacre. I heard stifled screams.

Why don't I do something?

Weak as I was, I made my way through the crowd, scrawny arms raised, but a couple of toughs at once picked me up and carried me across to a hillock, where I lay.

My followers were now encircled and were being shoved inwards with angry grunts and curses, with never ending kicks. Soon I could see nothing but a shell of gleaming backs, snuffing out the final resistance. When the circle opened up and the storm troopers retired, panting and disgusted (I suspected), the ground was covered with piles of limbs that swayed like seaweed in a dull liquid. I refused to accept it. No, I could not be guilty.

"Arise, O Lord! Confront them, overthrow them! Deliver my life from the wicked by thy sword!"

But a voice rose above the horror: "Blessed are they that suffer . . ."

I turned, appalled. Jesus was standing up on a dune, surrounded by the twelve. I thundered:

" 'The voice of one crying in the wilderness: Prepare ye the way of the Lord!' "

"Blessed are you when you are hounded and persecuted, for your reward in heaven shall be great!"

I fell on my kness in the bloodstained water and in that lucid moment wondered: "Aren't we preaching the same thing? Why do we persecute each other?"

Then I remembered his words some days before: "I

must abase myself that he may be exalted," and decided that I would abase myself, to further the triumph of Truth. No longer would I baptize, or put up resistance. Jesus would be the undisputed leader of the movement I had founded, and the fact that he was acting in bad faith made no difference. His words were divine.

As I stumbled out of the river I tried to make myself heard, shouting: "He who comes after me is stronger than me," but no one was listening. Some had fled, some, terrified by the truncheons, had gone across to Jesus, who was still speaking. Sunset came darkly, the low hills were streaked with groups limping home, supporting each other. Across the river the Roman campfires lit up.

Events moved fast and there is no point in my lingering over them. Worried by the unexpected attack, people came to me more than ever in the days that followed. They came to show the fidelity they had found again, and I wanted to shout: "Showing your loyalty won't save you. Fight evil with actions, not with protests!"

Instead, they wept, being so moved; some praised God, on the dunes. In the dead of night Jesus came to see me.

He spoke as if grieved and sincere. "You mustn't think I provoked that slaughter. It's the kind of thing that's a part of setting an armed organization. It was the landowners' doing."

I made no answer. It no longer concerned me.

"We must come to an agreement to avoid further bloodshed," he continued. "I'm retiring."

I looked up at him, surprised.

"That way, at least you'll believe me," he said.

He kissed my hand and vanished. And indeed, tents

and fences were taken up. For a moment I had the illusion my old glade had been restored to the past. I was so moved that I knelt down to pray. It had all happened so suddenly, in the first light of dawn, that it made the place look unreal. Even the people, who flocked in at sunrise, looked about them astonished. But I was not yet preaching.

The news that Zaccharius, Timothy and Jonathan were not to be found was brought to me by Naab, at night, in a hurry. Completely soaked from the rain, he crept up to my tent.

"It's Naab," he panted. They had taken them away the day before, and were looking for him as well; he had come to warn me. I tried to make him stay, so that I could give him food and get him dry, but he was so scared that he slipped away like a ghost. That's how we'll all end up, I thought.

Events spurred me into going outside. I thundered out my old, simple words with the enthusiasm of a believer going to his martyrdom. I now know this feverish activity was just my last song. At first people listened to me with rapture, singing hymns and praises, then diligently, in silence; then numbers fell off, and kept dwindling.

"They've killed Zaccharius," Elifaz murmured to me, in a moment's pause. I looked at those left in the glade, at the faces of men who were still ashamed to abandon me though in their hearts they knew that sooner or later they too would do so. "They found his body in a sewer, with the hands and feet tied."

I saw two or three men stir on the fringes of the small crowd, and move away. Timothy and Jonathan were found drowned in the Dead Sea, and all trace of Naab was lost. Elon managed to escape, I know.

But before they came to arrest me officially, a crowd appeared on the hill, covering it gradually like a layer of wool. The people came down towards the river, and at their head I saw a figure dressed in white, which I recognized as Jesus when they reached the glade. He took no notice of me but went to the river, stood in it and vigorously began to baptize, making the gray day luminous. People went into the water filled with joy, singing, embracing each other, kissing Jesus' garments.

At the midday meal, while they were all sitting on the grass, eating the food that was distributed free, he preached. Again I heard the subject I knew so well, and once again I was subdued by its irresistible truth. Looking at Jesus from a distance I said to myself: "Why not shout: 'Behold the Lamb of God, behold him who takes away the sins of the world!' "

And indeed, supported by Elifaz and Natan, hands outstretched and swaying with weakness after my involuntary fast, I walked forward. When people recognized me the entire crowd turned and, as if surprised to see me, Jesus himself pronounced the words I had been considering a moment earlier:

"Behold the Lamb of God, behold him who takes away the sins of the world!"

Mild as a lamb led to the slaughter, I let him lead me into the crowd, let myself be displayed, pointed at, lifted up, applauded. I recognized many faces of those I had baptized, I saw Peter smiling kindly at me as if I were a forgiven child, and the other eleven watching me calmly, tolerantly. I wanted to speak, but no longer had the strength to.

"Everything's going fine, you know," Jesus confided to

me later, before he left. I saw a metallic gleam in his beautiful eyes. He was already on his way, waving his hand at me as if I were any poor soul.

When I saw spears moving on the brow of the hill, I realized that the end had come. The squad of guards stopped before my tent and Herod's officer showed me the warrant for my arrest. Natan, in his simplicity, leapt forward brandishing a kitchen knife, and, no doubt without meaning to, cut off the ear of one of the guards. A sword ran through him and he died like a poor good goat, half-shutting his eyes that were still gazing at me. Elifaz came along behind, helping me, but when we reached Herod's fortress at Machero, he was taken away and I have seen nothing of him since, dear, faithful friend.

I was kept in an underground cell for three days before a court official came down to see me. Preceded by two men holding torches and followed by an escort of guards wearing helmet and breastplate, he peered into the darkness until he could see my face, and when he saw it he drew back. I can hardly have been an appealing sight. From the moment I had seen a man run through before my eyes I had lived in a kind of dream. The officer unrolled the parchment and read it. I was accused of sedition, blasphemy, conspiracy against the state and calumny. I gave no answer.

After another three days, two guards, holding me up, took me outside. I saw the sunlight and realized how beautiful life could be. A chariot was waiting for me. I was taken to the nearby hot springs and plunged in. This restored me, and I realized my austere life on the banks of the Jordan had been pleasant. When a slave cut my hair and beard and another dressed me in clean clothes I did not resist. I wore a pair of soft sandals, too, and when I was taken back to the fortress I did not refuse a decent meal served to me on the terrace of the tower that looked out over the Dead Sea.

It was sunset. A sound of panting made me turn, and a head poked up from the steps. Breathing hard, Herod climbed up and came to sit on a stone pediment in front of me. He got his breath back and we looked at each other without speaking.

"You're John the Baptist," he began. "I came to hear you one day, I mixed with the crowd. I liked you."

I did not answer. I had eaten, I felt clean, I was breathing fresh air. He noticed my state of feebleminded euphoria and smiled in a melancholy way.

"We're all of us men," he said. And he added surprisingly: "Even God. But what is it you want, from men and from God? Don't think I want to persecute you. On the contrary, I want to help you if I can. What is it you want?"

I answered slowly, because of my weakness, that my preaching was compatible with that of the prophets, which meant it could not mean sedition or blasphemy or conspiracy against the state, and least of all calumny. In any case, calumny against whom?

"I have been told," said Herod, looking at the floor, as if it was an effort to say it, "that when you preached you railed personally against me. Because of my marriage to my sister-in-law."

I tried not to show surprise.

"You made a great mistake," he went on, without conviction. "Why did you do it?"

"You know," I replied, "that I care nothing about you or

your wife or any one man, and that I have never preached against any individual man."

"But it's said you do."

"It must suit someone, then," I said sadly, having already realized who it might be. Herod was uneasy. He leaned towards me a little.

"Why don't you leave the country? Why not go to Greece or Alexandria? You could live there undisturbed. This may be your own country, but this age doesn't suit you. Go and live in some civilized, sophisticated, tolerant society, where faith means culture. Here, in this dry, God-obsessed country, every man's a wolf to his neighbor."

"God," I replied, "manifests himself to wolves in particular. Do you know Jesus?"

I saw Herod sigh deeply. "That wolf," he murmured.

"He preaches words inspired by God," I continued. "He says it isn't the healthy who need God, but the sick. Our country is sick."

"Do you mean the oppression of the Romans?"

I shook my head.

"I mean the sickness of ignorance. Our country hasn't yet realized that oppression doesn't come from outside, but from our own conscience. Outwardly, man has always been oppressed. Do you know Jesus well?"

He did not answer. I went on:

"He speaks inspired words. It is he who will save our country, all countries, all men."

"How do you know?"

At last we looked into each other's eyes and smiled as brothers:

"Because Jesus will pay with his life too, like me. He

has betrayed me into your hands and in his turn he'll be betrayed by you. Without knowing it he's done the will of God. My martyrdom will count for nothing. Jesus' martyrdom will count because only his words are divinely inspired."

"How can it be," said Herod darkly, "that a diabolical man can speak words that are divinely inspired?"

"This is what I've been wondering myself, this is what's been tormenting me, but I've stopped wondering, I've decided to accept him as he is. I love Jesus, the man who has betrayed me and who will have me killed. I love my betrayer because his words help me to live and will help me to die."

I was led back to my cell, where I am now, for another few hours. I am giving what I am writing to one of the guards. The Zealots have tried to assassinate Jesus, without success. Herod urged me to leave the country, but I refused. I have come to the conclusion that what they really want me to do is disappear. Alive, I would always be a possible threat; dead, I shall be forgotten, or at most remembered. I am not afraid to die, though I love life, and through it, God.

I hear news of riots, arrests, and persecutions instigated by Jesus. They no longer concern me. I live on his word and I have overcome pain. He, the man himself, came to see me yesterday. His metal eyes, that when he wishes can show such sweetness, shut his soul behind an iron veil. He was impenetrable.

"Why have you come?" I asked him.

"Because with you a part of me is going," he replied.

"If you feel any remorse, don't. You've done what you

had to do. What you do is wrong, as all our actions are. But your thought is right, as our thought always is. The people, whom you are betraying, will not become meek and mild to suit the landowners and Herod and the Romans. Their weakness will demolish the powerful, the bullies, the wicked. And it is your thought that will bring about this victory. Doing wrong, you have done right."

He stared at me without moving, and in the wavering light of the torches his hair, with its dark gleans, was still as in a painting.

"They will say all kinds of things about me," he said, "and many of them invented. But I know that one man, you, understood me. This is why a part of me goes with you."

I kissed the hem of his garment, he laid a hand on my head, turned, and left. The light touch of that hand has grown, and weighs on me like a great stone, trying to crush me, blot me out. I am dying for having believed in this man, and I believe in him still. Oh Lord, make Jesus true. Through the bars of my cell I look at the sea gull, which after so long has turned up again. Perched on the highest point of the fortress in the moonlight, it is the only patch of white in all this blue.

PART TWO

The
Testimony
of
Judas
called
Iscariot

THE TESTIMONY OF JUDAS, CALLED ISCARIOT. I am setting down my evidence so that in the future at least people will know what happened. At present they despise me.

I remember the day I was put up for the office of party treasurer. They had met in Peter's house at Capharnaum, in Galilee. I was brought in. They were sitting at a long table.

"Our brother Jacob," Jesus said, "is for health reasons obliged to give up the job of treasurer. I wish to thank him, express appreciation for the responsible and efficient way he has carried out his duties, and wish him a speedy recovery; and at the same time I propose that our candidate Judas Iscariot take over for him."

And with a gesture he introduced me. The other twelve murmured their agreement.

I had been in the party some time and was already on friendly terms with more than one member of the executive. Peter liked me and on the whole they approved of me. The one who still kept me at a distance was Jesus, who, although socially the same as the rest, kept himself aristocratically withdrawn. For this reason I thought it proper, out of respect for the leader, to list my qualifications.

"I've been bookkeeper for a number of firms, I've had a long spell as a Temple tax collector, I speak Latin, and I've had some success with agricultural business deals."

Not knowing what else to add, I was silent. Jesus noticed my embarrassment and nodded approval. Jacob, rising wearily from his seat (he died two months later), insisted on my taking it. Everyone clapped. That was how I began.

With surprise I realized that Jesus was taking notice of me. At first I thought it was because I was humble and physically handicapped. I now know that the way he kept gazing at me expressed the curiosity of the intellectual who saw in me his opposite.

One day when we were alone in the office and I was doing the accounts he said:

"I don't in the least doubt your vocation to our idea," and

he spoke slowly, considering me through scholarly, half-shut lids, "but what brought you to us?"

I've never had the gift of expressing myself in words. I replied: "I don't know. I liked it. I mean, I started poor. I have nothing. And this is the party of the poor, isn't it?"

He went on staring as if I were some curious object, while I went back to totaling my figures. It was one of the days he seemed bored. He would yawn, drop his chin on his chest, and do nothing.

Some time later he asked me, as if in his sleep:

"What do you think of our movement? Is it making headway?"

I looked up from the register and exclaimed: "Just look at the number who contribute to it!"

He pretended to be interested and I gave him a detailed report, with all the figures neatly arranged, credit and debit, and the difference that meant a profit. To impress him I used technical terms. But he was no longer listening.

He got up, and banged his fist on the table.

"But nobody talks about us! In Jerusalem they don't even know we exist, and here in Galilee they don't take us seriously. Then in my hometown I can't even go into the square without all of them laughing at me. This isn't the party of the poor or the rich, it should be everyone's party, otherwise it's no good."

He slammed shut the account book and hissed through his teeth: "It's always a matter of money. Always!"

At that time I still took no active part in things. Jesus arranged what was to be done and each man went off to preach. We had our meals together, except for Jesus, and lived with our own families. Jesus stayed with Peter and spoke in public only on Sundays. Other days he read, or lazed, or had odd meals all alone. Or else he became wildly restless and went for four-hour walks. From these he came back worn out and bad-tempered.

We made no headway. The idea of redeeming our people, all people, through love and altruism, of treating Romans as brothers, fired nobody. Some said: "It's all ancient history" and quoted Isaiah, Jeremiah, Ezekiel, even the Law. Unless Jesus spoke. Then they argued. I ventured to say to him:

"You should speak more often. That's the way to get to them, you know."

Lying on the sofa, he opened his eyes and replied:

"What can you talk about to a people indoctrinated by two thousand years of empty talk? They're so busy worrying about the flies they don't notice the wolves."

He got up, shook his hair, tidied his clothes, climbed on to a stool and broke into one of his splendid improvised speeches. He was bursting with ability. I longed to be a thousand, a hundred thousand listeners. Trembling with secret enthusiasm, I settled down to the accounts again. It was then that I remembered my son, who had died as a boy ten years before, and thought that he would now have been the same age as Jesus.

❁    ❁    ❁

We made no headway but we carried on. We were one of many movements for freedom of the spirit which the Romans tolerated and the priests in the Temple mocked. But we had something the others lacked: a leader of great personality. I knew that some day he would be widely known. I wondered whether what happened to a man depended entirely on others or not.

"We're getting more supporters, you know," I would tell him when we were alone, exaggerating. He never even glanced at the accounts.

"A slavish, apathetic people, that cares nothing for politics!" he raged. "An executive bursting to have its little say! They copy what I say and then come along to me and tattle about one another! Every one of them would like to take over for me and give the orders!"

I began making inquiries, secretly. Starting with Peter, I asked him what he thought of the party.

"With him expecting manna from heaven," he said, nodding to indicate Jesus, "I've no idea what we'll come to. Do you think he ought to lie around as he does? The rest of us get about, preach, keep on the move—at least I do. But what about him? This is getting us nowhere. And it's costing me plenty, too."

I asked Matthew.

"What do you want me to say?" he replied. "It's going the way it's going. But things will improve, I've a feeling. It's all a matter of being able to wait." He lowered his voice. "But don't you think there's a lack of coordination? Take Peter, now: what does he do to justify being deputy-leader? And what about the others, why don't they do their homework? There are too many amateurs around, I'd say."

Thomas was elusive. Simon shook his head violently and refused to answer, but gave me a meaning look. Thaddeus talked at length about his plans and ended up:

"Then things would start moving."

John, being young and amusing, gave the best answer:
"The party's all right, otherwise the party would be over."

So we carried on, wave-tossed on a gray shoreless sea. I was worried by the impatience and restless boredom of Jesus, and in order to cheer him I became his audience. He would talk to me for hours.

But then he would lose confidence and spend a whole afternoon gazing out of the window, with his head in his hands. I asked him if I might preach myself. He shrugged. I went.

I had chosen a Sunday evening, in a small square with a quiet inn. I had brought a wooden box with me and when I had climbed onto it I was silent. People gathered. Some were already making fun of me. It hurt me to stand up straight and stiff-legged on such a small surface.

"Blessed are the meek, the oppressed and they that thirst for justice," I began, too quickly, "for theirs is the Kingdom of Heaven."

Hearing me stammer, someone laughed. I had never spoken in public and for the first time I realized how hard it was to maintain a rhythm. I raised my voice.

"It has been said . . ."

"If it's been said," the same interrupted, "why say it again?"

I thought of Jesus as a son watching his father made ridiculous. My chin trembled.

"It has been said: woe to you who now laugh, because you shall suffer and weep!"

There were exclamations of protest, and some pushed forward, warding off what I had said. Confusedly I repeated what Jesus had said:

" 'If you love only those that love you, what merit is there? Even the sinners love those that love them.' "

Here I tripped up and went on:

" 'Whereas if you love those that hate you, what won't those that love you feel for you? And if you don't love those that love you, how will those that have always loved you and can no longer love you, love you?' "

I didn't know what I was saying and, with the tension, my leg felt as if it had turned to stone.

" 'Judge not,' " I shouted at the top of my voice, " 'and you shall not be judged! Hypocrite, first take the beam out of you own eye!' "

Two youngsters started looking in each other's eyes. They pretended to have seen the beam, and one of them, shoving his knee on the other's chest, was laboriously pulling it out. Then they heaved it on to their shoulders and began carrying it away while the rest of the audience, folded up with laughter, peered into one another's eyes as they had done. The square was filled with fun and good humor, and others were drawn into it from the alleyways around.

I yelled:

" 'Can the blind lead the blind?' "

"No!"

" 'Won't they both fall in the ditch?' "

"Yes!"

They pretended to be blind, held hands, and rolled about on the ground. The innkeeper had emerged and was bustling about. Stupidly I shouted my last sentence, even stumbling over a word:

" 'And if they strike you on the cheek, turn the other cheek!' "

There was a roar of laughter. Everywhere there were cheeks being slapped, eyes freed of beams, the blind led about: I'd never seen such a racket. One man tripped me up. Another, remembering my advice, pulled off my clothes: then a couple of sandals stood in front of me. I recognized them and huddled up with shame, covering myself. Jesus climbed on to the box.

What came out of him to make the mob instantly quiet? He looked at them from above and started softly:

"Which of you, whose child asked for bread, would give him a stone?"

He pointed to me.

"Or if he asked for a fish, would give him a serpent?"

He roared:

"If you therefore, who are evil, know how to give good things to your children, how much more will your Father who is in heaven give to those that ask him! Do unto others as you would have done to you. For this is the law and the prophets!"

Silence froze the crowded square. They gazed after him as he moved away, disgusted.

"Idiot," he hissed at me coldly, as soon as we were back at headquarters. "This is the sort of trouble you make for me."

The executive was furious. Peter said to Jesus:

"We deplore the treasurer's action and ask for an assurance that the incident won't recur."

Simon was even more explicit.

"We have noticed a certain collusion between you and the treasurer. Is it just friendship, or is it patronage?"

One after another they spoke, excitedly. Jealousy oozed

from all they said. Then Philip, who usually spoke little (and for this reason I thought him the most dangerous), gave the final stab:

"I consider this personal relationship between our leader and an official harmful to the party's cause, so I'm asking for a vote of confidence in the treasurer."

I was asked to leave, and the executive arranged to meet an hour later. Peter managed to approach me.

"Don't worry," he told me kindly (at heart he was always the best of them), "you'll get off this time. But you must be more careful."

There were eight votes in my favor and four against me. From that moment I had a firm feeling that they were trying to discredit Jesus, and I decided to give my whole self to defending him.

❋　❋　❋

At the beginning of summer it was decided to launch a campaign in Jerusalem. Our funds were barely enough for it and I said so. It went very badly. The personal ambitions of Thaddeus, Simon and Philip, and the inefficiency of the others, including Peter, damaged our chances. The preaching was confused and muddy, without the slightly enigmatic intellectual lyricism that made Jesus so easy to listen to. Audiences fell away. Above all, money was so tight and so closely watched that I was unable to make proper arrangements. Sometimes meetings weren't even publicized in advance, and some of our contacts in Jerusalem weren't even warned in time.

"But what's Judas been doing?" I heard Thaddeus protest.

"Ask *him*," Simon answered, turning toward Jesus.

The evening before we went back to Capharnaum we all met for supper at the house of the agent, one Cleofas, a merchant and double-crosser (I later discovered that he was also in the pay of a nationalistic movement, inimical to us). Everything had been arranged to give the evening an air of confidence and to urge us to carry on. We were to discuss our mistakes frankly and recommend remedies. But everything went wrong. Philip started the argument even before we had begun eating.

"The party," he said, looking spiteful, "must be re-shaped."

No one replied, although everyone had understood. Jesus unfolded his napkin and spread it on his knees.

"Because, let's face it, there's a crisis of leadership." Philip went on. Then, turning to Jesus, he said, with his tight, cowardly, politician's smile: "Nothing personal, of course. It's the system I'm talking about."

"What system?" said Peter, chewing at a piece of bread. "No system will work if those who use it can't make it work."

"Meaning?" Simon asked dryly.

Peter looked round, and as the servants were beginning to ladle out the soup he replied:

"Meaning that before speaking in public you've got to practice, that before you deal with a subject you've got to understand it yourself, and that before you praise a principle you've got to believe in it. That's my meaning."

Philip breathed deeply, and all heads went down for the first mouthful.

"Exactly," he said. "Now who believes most in our

cause, the leader or his followers? That's what it all gets down to, I think. In other words, is our leader inspired enough to give his followers a sense of mission, or isn't he pretty much of a dead weight we're carrying?"

"I refuse to accept these insinuations!" Peter cried, wiping his mouth.

All three together, Philip, Simon and Thaddeus, said that their questions were perfectly proper. One or two others put in a word; no one listened. At the end of the table Andrew and John, the two youngest, followed it all without speaking. I heard John exclaim, with his usual wit:

"Blessed are they that hunger and thirst!" as he poured out a drink.

The meal and the good wine did away with argument and the party broke up into groups. Cleofas was efficient and hospitable and at the end I thanked him. But it was clear that after the supper things would never be the same again. I approached Jesus openly:

"Do you realize they're doing all they can to replace you?"

We were back at headquarters, in Capharnaum, and outside the countryside was dull. He looked up at me laconically from the Scriptures, without answering.

"What is it you need?" I asked him. "You can tell me, I'm old enough to be your father."

He got up and walked up and down, ruffling my gray hair with his hand.

"What is it I need? . . . money! Why don't you rob some caravan for me? Why don't you steal from the Temple!"

69

I stayed seated a long time, thinking over what he had said as a joke. But the idea of getting money for him had gotten to me, and never left me again.

* * *

It was a very beautiful spring, the shores of the lake were in bloom and at evening the sky was so blue that it seemed it would never grow dark. Jesus was planning a campaign in the whole of Galilee, and kept Nazareth, his hometown, for himself. I went along with him.

Things were worse than they had been in Jerusalem.

"Who do you think you are?" they shouted at him in the square.

"Play the great man somewhere else!"

Jesus had often said to me, with a kind of acid pleasure: "No one can ever preach in his own town, he'll never be believed, even by his own relations." But now, when I saw him withdraw, defeated, with a dog yapping after him, my heart was wrenched with pain. Once around the corner he ran down the hill and when he was out of the village dropped down on a rock, covering his face with his hands.

I panted up to him, my leg in agony. He drew away his hands. His face was dry and disgusted, and his eyes seemed to follow a retreating thought.

"And to think," he said, grimacing horribly, "that I had just one ambition: to become someone in my own town."

"What sort of mess have you gotten yourself into?" I murmured, already alarmed about what the executive would have to say. He had risen, and was drinking at a spring under a willow tree. As it was after midday I decided to go into town and buy food. After half an hour I was back. Jesus was no longer alone. A girl was with him. I approached them, hidden in the greenery, and stopped behind a bush.

"Of course I remember you, Dina!" Jesus was saying, and he touched her hand.

"You wanted to marry me," the girl said questioningly, and she sounded embarrassed. "Why did you make me think so?"

"I didn't know what I was saying."

There was a pause; then Jesus asked: "Did you happen to be passing, or did you come on purpose?"

"I came on purpose."

"How is my mother?"

"She's well. Why not come and see her?"

Jesus didn't answer. The girl went on:

"I still love you, but I can't wait forever. Have you really made up your mind?"

His voice sounded weak, and embarrassed too: "Yes."

"Well, that's that," said the girl, still standing there. I guessed her throat was choked and her eyes were swollen. Just then I longed for Jesus to say what any man would say and to draw her to him as I had done with my poor wife. And to say to her: "Let's be married, Dina, let's live together all our lives, with our children, in our own home."

"Dina, I can't."

"Well, if you can't, goodbye," she said, and took a step back. The tears started flowing. "That means I'll wait a bit longer."

Jesus said no more.

"It means that I shan't yet get married," she went on,

71

withdrawing farther. "I'll keep on thinking about you, and be patient."

Weeping she repeated: "Patient, that's what I'll be."

At last she turned and went towards the village, her shoulders shaking with sobs. Run after her, I prayed within me, there's the love you preach to others. Love her, even if you don't love her! When she had vanished I approached noisily, pretending to have just arrived. Jesus' eyes were glassy.

"Judas," he said, in what seemed like a whisper, "shall I ever succeed?"

I looked at him, stricken.

"I'm eaten up with ambition," he said, sounding choked, pressing his belly as if it hurt. He flung himself down on his back, looking up at the sky. "And nobody helps me."

I left him in that position, as if dead, for a couple of hours. When he got up he washed his face, and seeing the food laid on the grass seized it greedily, gulping it down eagerly. We set off at once for Capharnaum, and he walked behind me, swaying like a drunk.

The executive was indignant over what had happened at Nazareth.

"So we've reached the point where the dogs yap at us!" Philip laughed slyly.

"It's all because there's no joint decision taken on our activities," Simon said angrily.

"You shut up!" said Peter. "What happened at Nazareth just shows that the party leader's able to stir things up. I only wish something of the sort had happened at Jerusalem!"

Later, though, he impatiently confided in me:

"To be frank, I don't understand him! What did he want to go to Nazareth for? He knew it, didn't he?"

But as things turned out, Peter was right. What happened at Nazareth was discussed all over Galilee and Jesus was the center of attention. We began to get known. Cunningly manipulating, without actually falsifying, the books, I announced a considerable surplus. It was a fact that a wealthy group in Jerusalem, of Greek extraction, had made donations. A certain Erastos, a philosopher and, it was said, a distinguished authority on Socrates and Stoic Rationalism, had actually invited Jesus to give a lecture in Jerusalem.

"You should go," I said. But he seemed more indifferent than ever.

But on the following Sundays, when he spoke at Capharnaum, Chorazin, Bethseda and Hippos, he was a success. We pushed on to Gadara and Pella, in the heart of the Decapolis, where the Greek tradition was strong, and, coming back along the sea of Tiberias, ended up at Magdala.

Another aspect of his personality, misunderstood by all except me, was his sudden uncontrolled outburst of, say, eating, or buying himself clothes and luxuries. When we were alone at headquarters, he was quite capable of making me order a meal for six and eating it alone, wasting it. "Do you realize," I'd scold him in a fatherly tone, "that we're counting pennies to launch another campaign in Jerusalem?"

"Let me alone. I know what I'm doing."

He was now well-known enough to pick and choose

among his invitations to dinner, so he had three garments of the finest linen made, and three pairs of sandals embroidered with gold. More than once he came home hot-tempered. When Peter remarked on it he replied: "I know what I'm doing."

This was his answer to everyone. But Philip, as I had foreseen he would, raised the matter. As things were going well he did so cautiously.

"I consider," he said, speaking with the tacit approval of the whole executive, "that personal showiness is something we shouldn't yet be going in for. We should wait till we're politically more stable and, to be quite frank, financially better off."

He turned cunningly to me: "How does our treasurer justify certain special expenses, mentioned in his last report?"

"Yes, how?" said Thaddeus.

Even John wasn't joking, but looking at Jesus with harsh, youthful scorn.

Peter saved us from embarrassment by saying cheerfully that these expenses were justifiable for publicity when Jesus spoke to a bunch of half-wits.

"Will you all shut up about tomorrow—you're obsessed with it, mean-minded souls that you are! Do you find the fields bothering about what's coming, do you find them scraping and saving and working out their accounts? Yet look at their flowers. Forget tomorrow. There's something wrong with every day, whether God sends it or not."

Bored, he looked at us all and said, as he rose:

"Let tomorrow alone. Let me alone."

But as Philip went out he murmured to Thaddeus and

Simon, while the others listened: "He knows what he's doing! But the Scriptures are quite clear: Everything in its time and a time for everything. How about that?"

      ❀    ❀    ❀

We were now one of the most controversial parties in the land. The Pharisees criticized what they called our irreverence to the Scriptures and the Temple became worried. And when Jesus answered the invitation and went to Jerusalem to give the lecture, I learned that for some time even the Romans had been watching him. One of their informers, in the discussion after the lecture, asked Jesus how he could reconcile his prophecy of the Kingdom of God with the duty to pay taxes to Caesar. Were there two Caesars, and two Gods?

It was obviously provocation, so I prepared, without the smallest doubt, to enjoy the way Jesus would get the better of him. And indeed he flattened his questioner with his well-known talent for such things. "They can be reconciled perfectly well. Give to Caesar the things that are Caesar's, and to God the things that are God's."

Yet, to find out more, I started making inquiries. I discovered that one of the many anti-Roman movements was a cultrual one formed in Jerusalem, and that its headquarters was the house of this same Erastos, the rich intellectual who had invited Jesus. I decided to go and see him.

"We ought to keep up our contacts." Erastos was interested. "There's a friendly meeting at my house tomorrow evening. Why not come along too?"

I accepted at once, but since I had a definite object in

visiting him, I told him right out that our party needed funds. He smiled approvingly. His fine house, and easy manners, the whole atmosphere of the capital, made me bold.

"We have nothing, just a program," I went on. "And to spread it we need money."

I aimed high: "A hundred thousand shekels. For a start."

He lifted his chin, and grew serious. For some time, he told me reassuringly, he had had us in mind; it was now a question of going into things formally, but in any case it wasn't so much money that counted, as contacts.

We went to supper, Jesus, Peter and I, and found ourselves in the triclinium with about twenty people. Erastos was a generous host. His Socratic moral outlook was tempered by his delight in the good things of life. Above all, he was an Epicurean. At once we realized that although his house was wholly Roman in style, he enjoyed more than anything speaking ill of the Romans, and at dessert he made a long speech, to which his friends listened deferentially.

"These barbarians from abroad—all decked out in tinsel they stole from our civilization! In trying to advance themselves through it they will wipe out our ancient culture altogether! Isn't it time we had nothing more to do with them, and told them plainly to stick to their shields?"

I realized all this had nothing to do with Jesus, but when we took our leave I managed to remind our host respectfully of our financial difficulties. The way he had behaved made it clear to me that on ideological issues he was merely self-seeking—a man who was knowledgeable but untalented, and who enjoyed being donnish in his own drawing room. His wealth was inherited, so he had no notion of its value. He gave us money.

"Look," I said, when we were back at the hotel, and I had run to Jesus' room and found Peter there as well. I was holding the unfolded letter of credit I had just received up to them. It wasn't for a hundred thousand shekels, but for ten thousand, which I could cash at a Temple money changer's.

Jesus was quite unmoved. Peter was agog. He gazed at it, saying, "Well, there's no knowing what else we might get here!"

Clearly the news got around, because when we got back to Capharnaum we had other gifts of money from a number of organizations in Jerusalem, such as the Friends of Culture and the Philosophy Club, and even a modest but significant sum from an unknown organization that called itself Ethical Renewal.

"What's wrong with you?" I finally asked Jesus. He hadn't spoken for three days. The executive was growing impatient.

He agreed to preach at Caesarea. We were amazed at the crowd that gathered. He spoke of the humble, of the simple, of the oppressed, but in obscure and not very effective parables. Yet the seed had germinated, and it felt as if the plant itself were pushing up, irresistibly, from underground. He gave two other complicated talks that were also enthusiastically received.

"It's all very well," Peter confided in me, "but . . ."

I guessed what he was thinking.

"Why don't you speak frankly to him?" I said. He did

so at once and I stood behind the wall, at a point where it was thin enough for me to overhear.

"You can't remain detached indefinitely," I heard Peter say persuasively. "It's all very well so long as people interpret it as the expression of an enigmatic personality who has something deep to say. But there comes a point, believe me because I'm older than you, when people will want to hear you speak clearly. Otherwise we'll run the risk of becoming a cultural movement ourselves. A little club. A clique."

Jesus was silent. Then he replied, with a weariness that seemed to have gotten into his bones:

"My soul is sorrowful even unto death."

"I don't understand you," Peter muttered. "Till recently you were so sure of yourself. How is it you've suddenly . . ."

Jesus interrupted him: "But Peter, do you still not understand? Haven't you realized that people want facts and not words? And that the only fact that would delight that crowd of cowards would be to see me nailed up, and be able to say: The prophecy of Isaiah is fulfilled! 'Like the lamb led to the slaughter, like the dumb sheep before the shearers.'"

"You read too much Isaiah!" I heard Peter exclaim.

"And you don't read him enough! You're a bunch of cowards yourselves! What you want is a corpse on the cross so that you can beat your breasts. 'He was numbered among sinners, he who took away the sins of many.' You hypocrites, all you can reason with is the prophets!"

He went out, upset.

"But you're the one with the prophets on your brain!"

78

Peter shouted after him. "What's the matter with you? Have you decided to be the Messiah?"

"And what are you doing here?" said Jesus, stopping when he saw me with my ear to the wall. I fell on my knees, embracing him.

"Not me," I said, beseechingly. "You know I understood."

His chin trembled, and he ran his hand through my hair.

I turned on Peter: "You shouldn't have spoken to him like that!"

"But it's he that drags the words out of one!"

"All right, all right, but you mustn't hurt him!"

Peter, who was a heftier man than I was, came up and stared at me.

"What is there between you and him?"

"I could be his father."

"That we know. But what's there between you?"

I too went out. At our meeting that evening the executive was icy. Peter was now hostile as well. Philip, Thaddeus and Simon played on this.

"To think we'd planned to intensify our campaign because things were going our way," Philip said spitefully. "Must we go back to where we were two years ago, unknown, ridiculous, just because our leader won't observe party discipline, which applies to him as well as the rest of us?"

"I object!" I shouted. Everyone turned to me, astonished.

"The treasurer is requested not to interfere in the discussion of plans," said Philip.

"I'm a member of the executive, you know!"

He was forced to sit down, which he did, with a snigger. And I spoke up in defense of Jesus, tangling my words, as usual, but ending with this warning:

"Why are you wondering what's to be done now? Didn't he found the party? Don't try to topple the leader. If there's a leader, you have to trust him, or what's the point of his being leader? You might as well change the leader: out with Jesus, and take on a new one!"

Jesus smiled at my lack of experience.

"It looks as though one of you will betray me," he said, ironically.

He gazed at me insistently, mocking me. I realized he was joking.

"All right, it'll be me," I said, laughing. And everyone laughed. On that note the meeting broke up. Philip teased me, but cordially:

"When you've something to say, always say the opposite of what you really mean!"

But what I had hoped for didn't happen.

As the party's popularity grew, Jesus remained angrily and scornfully indifferent. The quarrel with Peter, I felt, had flung him into despair.

He looked liverish. I could see his stifled ambition, and it hurt me to see him chafing.

"Why not get married?" I asked him.

He stared at a distant point in the landscape, where the purple was turning to the blackness of night.

"It would be good for you," I went on. "Basically, a man needs a woman to advise him. And a married man can get further in politics—it looks more respectable, more moral."

He looked at me with disgust.

The others were growing more hostile toward me. And yet they had never had a treasurer like me. The party funds were well invested, and were already bringing in an income of at least twenty percent. I bought a building and resold it a week later at almost double the price. I lent money at fifty percent interest and brazenly lent to contractors working on fortifications for the Romans, at the greediest interest rates I could get. I didn't care. The party needed money and I took it wherever it came from, whatever it was for, at whatever interest I could get.

The day came when I could announce proudly to the executive:

"We're in a position to bear the cost of a political campaign anywhere in the country, without worrying about funds. Our investments will more than make up the balance."

But Jesus was still sulking. To coax him out of it I bought him clothes and fine food, and finally decided on a secret experiment: I brought him a woman.

I ordered a meal and left them alone. Some time later, I pushed open the door. Jesus was where I left him; he hadn't moved. The woman was on her knees praying. I pulled her up by the arm.

She was shaking her head through her tears and seemed carried away. As she composed herself she said: "No one ever spoke to me before. I didn't know such words existed."

What was it that was urging Jesus to degenerate, just when his remarkable powers of persuasion had ripened and we were on the point of breaking through? Was it a crisis of faith in himself and in his own ideas, or a crisis of fear, the fear of becoming a victim of the masses, an object of prophecy, as he had shouted to Peter? The news that

81〕

John, son of Zachary, called the Baptist, had been be-
headed by Herod at the wish of the Romans, made him
close up in an even gloomier silence, broken only by the
violent shaking of his shoulders.

We still had donations, and invitations to give lectures.
Nothing improved things. Twice an audience gathered to
hear Jesus speak, but he failed to appear.

"Well, we certainly can't go on like this," Peter announced. He was looking meaningly at Philip and I
shivered. Five of us were in my office and Jesus was
sleeping in his room. Peter turned to me: "Tell us everything."

And I told them all I thought I knew: that Jesus had
given way to a form of self-destruction, denial of life,
disgust in men.

"He's going through a phase of inner renewal, and he'll
come out of it a new man," I said. "Through the aberra-
tions of his body he's purifying his soul. It's just a matter
of waiting."

"But how long?" Peter said impatiently.

"And how can we put across a party without an effective
leader?" said Philip, already exploiting the situation.

I was racing round the room like a rat in a trap. "There
is a leader," I exclaimed.

"But where?"

With all the energy I could gather I went to see Jesus.

"You disgust me!" I shouted at him, with an old man's
scorn. His face was worn, his mouth red; his eyes were
dull.

"And I don't mind telling you: you disgust me!"

But, as I had foreseen, I yielded to tenderness. I seized

€ 82

one of his hands, put it to my cheek, and, weeping with rage and feeling, said:

"Don't you realize they're trying to get rid of you? Your career, your future, all you've studied, your talent!"

I reminded him of the scene with Dina, of the way he had given up everything in order to succeed, his admission that that was all he wanted. And now that he had it within reach, he was refusing it. Where was he going, where?

Dully, he replied:

"Where you cannot come."

The whole night I spent in terror. Every ten minutes I got up to go in and take a look at him. After four in the morning I dozed off, and must have been sleeping for half an hour when I awoke with a start. I ran in to him. His bed was empty. My heart was bursting as I rushed into the garden and called him softly, to avoid waking anyone: "Jesus, Jesus!"

I stumbled against his body, and stifled a cry. He was swinging.

Stretching my leg out sideways for fear it would break, I heaved hard and lifted him. In that terrible position I stayed for at least ten minutes. Then I managed to loosen the noose and slowly, breaking a nail, undo the knot. He fell, dragging me with him. It was dawn and a white dove was cooing in the apple tree.

I kept it secret from the others. And when he awoke in bed I said nothing to him, in fact I spoke in a practical tone, reminding him that tomorrow was Sunday and it would be time for him to take up his activities again.

"Now," I said, giving him some barley water, "you're cured, aren't you?"

It did not seem strange to me that he slowly regained his

color and began to renew his contacts with others. The terrible crisis was overcome and I never spoke to him about it. But Peter still brooded, and those who backed Philip were silent, which was more dangerous than if they had spoken. It was in this atmosphere of cold opposition that Jesus, still weak, went out on a hill where they were gathering the grape harvest and gave the sermon I think was his most successful, the one that began:

"Blessed are the poor in spirit, for theirs is the Kingdom of Heaven."

It was a new man speaking. We all, without saying so, understood at last what had been the real reason for his crisis. The concepts were those he had always expressed, and were taken from the Scriptures, but now he enlarged on them, illustrated them, and the whole ideological design opened up like a firmament in which the ideas were balanced and formed a perfect system. God appeared to everyone as even more than universal. For the first time we felt with absolute certainty that God was within us, that God and man were the same thing. So freedom must be that of the soul, not of the country: since there were neither countries nor men, but a single country and a single Man. Even the Romans were our brothers.

The vintagers, having listened in silence, went back to pick the grapes, settling them lovingly in their baskets. Without speaking, they smiled. I walked beside Jesus, hurrying to keep up with him, and he smiled at me, happy as a child. Need I hide the fact that my throat felt choked all the way?

But next day a delegation of Zealots turned up at our headquarters, asking to speak to the leader. There were three of them and they came from Galilee, where the

Irredentist movement was strong. Peter, Philip, Thaddeus, and, nearest of all, John, as if he were his bodyguard, were grouped round Jesus.

"We don't approve of your program," said one of the three, looking Jesus in the face.

"I know," Jesus answered. "And I don't approve of yours."

"We must avoid an internal struggle that would weaken us both," the man went on.

"It won't happen," said Jesus.

The leader of the delegation said that on the contrary, it was inevitable. The Zealots refused to countenance weakness and would hound our feeble, defeatist party till it broke up. The Scriptures had forbidden the liberation of foreigners. God had thus commanded his people.

"I am God," Jesus answered.

Everyone froze. Philip shook his head and looked at the three men as if to say: "He's mad."

"We don't care who you are," their leader said. "What worries us is that you're doing what we don't want you to do."

Jesus smiled ironically and answered:

"You think I have come to bring peace on earth! I have not come to bring peace, but the sword. I have come to divide son from father, daughter from mother, daughter-in-law from mother-in-law; a man's family will become his enemies. My sword is sharper than yours."

And seizing the knife that stuck out of the tunic of one of them, he hurled it on the table. The Zealots backed away from him. Jesus picked up the knife, gave it back, and, with a loving kiss on the cheek, led them out.

"Magnificent!" John gave a leap of enthusiasm: "An-

swer like that if you can!" he said to Philip, shoving him
teasingly.

"Playing on words!" Philip protested furiously.

Peter was moved, and when Jesus came in said: "You
were splendid! Hey, women—bring something to drink!"

"What do they mean, in practice?"

A lively discussion followed, but although most of the
others were on our side I could not fail to notice that
another two, Thomas and Bartholomew, had gone over to
the opposition.

The party was split. When I presented my three-
monthly report I took the chance of reproaching Philip's
supporters with this. The assets I declared made Peter puff
out his cheeks and even Jesus look up; then I added:
"Those who use other people's ideas without contributing
anything to the party's program would do just what I've
done."

Thaddeus realized what I was implying and shouted:
"Here, you mind your own business!"

"Just what I'm doing," I retorted. "It's you that made
me pay a bill there was no need for. Your meeting at
Tiberias last week was pointless! You repeated exactly
what Jesus had said."

"Because I'm loyal to the party!"

"But in private you and the others like you never stop
running down your leader. Why can't you think of something new?"

There was an outburst of anger.

"No one invented the party's ideas!" shouted Philip, on
his feet.

"They're the ideas of Jesus, his alone!" I yelled from the
opposite side.

"The party manifesto," he cried, but the row had grown too deafening, "doesn't belong to anyone! It belongs to us all!"

Later Jesus spoke to me.

"Don't annoy him," he said. "I have a comfortable majority."

"But it might get smaller," I said; I was worried.

He shook his head, sure of himself.

❋   ❋   ❋

Having money meant more action. We began a second campaign in Jerusalem, and this time, thanks to the support of several friendly organizations, it was carefully planned. Philip's supporters, I must admit, collaborated usefully. Erastos sent a delegation to meet Jesus at our hotel. A public discussion was held, in which Jesus kept his statements vague, and said our party stood for peace and order. One of Erastos's henchmen murmured in his ear and next time he replied Jesus managed a reluctant:

"We're planning the country's cultural renewal, of course—a whole new concept of culture."

Someone in the audience (sent by the Romans, no doubt) asked:

"Would the teaching of Latin be obligatory?"

Only I could read the patient twist on Jesus' face as he replied:

"We consider the Latin culture an integral part of our national life."

He first spoke on the peristyle of Erastos' house. It was crowded with a smart invited audience of people standing about among the pillars. A capital city's a whole new world! The questions asked were sharp and quick, and no

87

one seemed surprised at anything. At first I was afraid Jesus might look like a bumpkin. But no. He was relaxed and confident as he answered, glancing from one to the next. From the way the meeting broke up, I realized it had been a success.

Erastos confirmed this loudly at supper.

"To our national emancipation through culture!" he said, raising his chalice to drink to Jesus.

Jesus spoke again in a square where the Roman police allowed meetings and free speech. But this time less successfully. There were too many people, and the sides of the square gradually filled with legionaries. A group of hecklers (Zealots, of course) kept interrupting Jesus, recalling the national uprising twenty years before to avoid paying tribute to a Roman Emperor, when Sulpicius Quirinus was Roman representative in Syria.

"Shut up and get moving!" they shouted.

Erastos himself advised Jesus to put off the talk authorized for the following day in a Temple courtyard. An important Roman official who was a useful man to know had dropped a hint. That same evening an officer of the Antonia Tower turned up at our hotel. He spoke our language well, and was civilized and extremely polite.

"We don't want to hinder free speech," he said diplomatically. "But there's public order to think of. Would it be too much to ask you not to speak in public places?"

"But the Temple is the Temple," said Peter.

The officer nodded, and answered with a smile which, given his Latin accent, looked imperious:

"Then let's put it this way: in the Temple you won't be speaking to the public, you won't hold any meetings, you'll just be speaking to the bystanders. How about that?"

We met in Jesus' room, puzzled. Philip was in favor of going right ahead. For once I said I agreed with him.

Peter was silent. Then he said: "Obviously we came here to do something."

He looked at Jesus and asked him: "What's your idea?"

We went into the Temple separately. Although we had decided to avoid holding meetings we had still failed to realize that in Jerusalem the smallest thing could flare up into trouble. In the Gentiles' courtyard Jesus was immediately recognized and the people crowded around him. I tugged at his clothes and murmured "The police," but it was no good. He became excited. And when he had one of his violent outbursts against the Temple authorities, calling them negligent reactionaries who were ruining the country because they couldn't get it into line with modern times, the police broke in, batons whirling, and troops of legionaries swooped down from the Antonia Tower, lances ready. Scared, the money changers shut up shop at once and left the place empty. The first stone flew. Then, like water flooding through a breached dyke, everything collapsed. I was just in time to see Jesus carried away.

We met again in the hotel, Peter with a black eye, Philip with a couple of broken ribs, John with a head injury and the others all more or less beaten up. Next morning Jesus joined us, brought along by two policemen, with orders to leave Jerusalem immediately.

The officer who had come two days before came in, and, amiable as ever, but accepting no objections, told us, as if he just happened to come along:

"Do whatever you like in Galilee but don't set foot in the capital. You see what can happen nowadays."

As he took leave of Jesus he said softly, whether diplomatically or seriously I don't know:

"Personally I agree with your party. You're perfectly right."

And, cloak fluttering, he disappeared.

They had banned us from Jerusalem but not from Judea. We decided at once to carry on our campaign there. Instead of going back to Capharnaum we stopped at Arimathea, where one of our firmest supporters lived, a rich landowner called Joseph. He gave us the use of a whole house and, talking incessantly, we got busy. Our internal quarrels seemed far away. Jesus carried us along with him.

One after another, we covered all the towns of Judea. Jesus pushed on as far as Hebron, and, skirting the capital, went over to Bethany.

But news of this reached Jerusalem, with immediate results. A Roman centurion came to see us, to remind us of the order to limit our activity to Galilee. We ignored the order and went to Jaffa. Here they had already been told of our presence in the district, so we left at once for Sichar. But that was no better and we decided to go still further north, stopping at Sebaste. Here, too, it was not long before a centurion came along to see us, so we felt it was unwise to stay in a town at all. We scattered about the slopes of Mount Gerizim, and split up among a number of shepherds' hamlets.

But, thus isolated, what could we do? Our discomforts, including physical ones, depressed us again. Philip turned on Jesus for his thoughtlessness in preaching in the Temple.

"It was just one of those things," Peter said, trying to restore calm.

"But when he insists on going his own way, it's always the same!" retorted Philip.

"And it's we who pay for it," Thaddeus added.

The very fact that we had been forced into isolation meant we had to overcome it. We tried out a series of quick talks with the local people and found the response was good. There were small outbursts and a party of Romans patrolling our villages found us determined to hold out. There was nothing else we could do.

"Suppose they arrest you someday?" I murmured to Jesus.

He looked at me, biting his nails. "If only they would," he said, as if to himself.

In a flash I understood.

"You mean that would be the one way to establish yourself?"

He looked at me without saying yes or no. But I had understood.

❁ ❁ ❁

So we decided to make another bid in Jerusalem.

To cover our tracks we stayed in various hotels and spoke at inn dining rooms and markets, to small groups in the squares; the police were unaware of us. One of us risked going into the Temple and reported that all was quiet.

Jesus went along there. Four guards at once tagged along behind and told him to keep moving. He came back to the hotel certain that the police would come and warn us to leave. But they didn't.

"Why?" I asked, feeling suspicious.

He was walking nervously round the room. "They don't want to make an issue of it," he said.

But Philip's supporters protested:

"We shall all end up inside!"

Even Peter suggested greater caution. But, unknown to us all, Jesus went back to the Temple and spoke to the people there. Two hours later the police came to the hotel. To our disappointment they were quite brief and simply advised us in a fatherly way not to set foot there again.

"You must realize you're risking us all," Peter told Jesus.

Even I ventured to say: "Don't push things too hard."

"You too!" he cried impatiently.

"Don't let this craze to assert yourself betray you," I said, urgently. "You'll make it, don't worry!"

But he went back to the Temple and this time openly addressed the crowd. By the time I arrived, panting, it was impossible to get into the Gentiles' courtyard, and the other entrances were blocked. The Antonia Tower seemed to me to be wrapped in the calm before the storm. But nothing happened, yet.

It became clear to us all, including Philip, that the Temple was getting the better of us by taking no notice. We decided to push on and provoke them. While Jesus was speaking in one place, Peter and John were speaking in another. This was repeated for five days on end. On the sixth, a Sunday, a Temple emissary finally came to see us.

"Your subversive activity won't do any of us any good, you know," he said courteously. "We think the only way to keep the Romans happy is to avoid upsetting the status quo. Urging the people to await the Kingdom of God, to repudiate the Temple, to consider all men as brothers, isn't the sort of thing that they tolerate. You fellows from the provinces don't know them. Believe me, they're fair and tolerant as long as they're not disturbed. Then they lash out mercilessly. Don't go telling them we're all brothers: they'll be annoyed. They're on top, remember."

He left, recommending us to confine our activity to private meetings. "Like those at Erastos' house, for instance," he added, with a small ironic smile.

When we were alone Peter exclaimed: "They haven't understood a thing! Our program of universality, of transcending nationalism! We've been talking to the air!"

Jesus closed himself into so gloomy a silence that I began to tremble for him. Things were coming to a head again.

"You're not going to be discouraged by small setbacks like these," I scolded him. "Did you think it would be easy to establish yourself? Why, it takes centuries, sometimes, to get a single idea understood."

He flung himself on the bed, his head buried in the pillow, and so I left him, as if destroyed.

He stayed shut up in his room for a week, and when he came out he looked like a ghost. He walked through the crowded streets and I saw him as just another man like the rest, and wondered if it wouldn't be better for him to be just like that. Why give up everything for a success that seemed illusory? On the other hand, how could an inspired intellectual adapt himself to lead an ordinary life?

He pressed his hands to his temples and confided in me.

"I can't go on," he said. "Something must happen. I need certainty."

I didn't know what to answer him.

But the most serious thing was that, besides all this, we had financial difficulties that I alone knew of, and these would soon become decisive. I figured out how we stood. Our funds were fast diminishing, I could have liquidated our invested capital, but this was the final remedy. The groups we were friendly with, which had helped us so far, after the Temply emissary's visit stopped doing so. Erastos still helped a little, then he too stopped. To economize we moved to Bethany, only three miles from the capital.

But, again, what were we to do there?

It was then that I decided to put my plan into action, the plan that made the name of Judas so much reviled.

❋   ❋   ❋

I brooded over it for a long time and I still maintain it was the most realistic, and the only one worth trying. I went to see Caiaphas, the Chief Priest, and spoke frankly: our party needed money; in exchange for financial help we would, for the time being, cease our subversive activity.

"A hundred thousand shekels."

He smiled, and shook his head: "A hundred thousand or a million, what's the use? You all come asking me for money. But what are you aiming at?"

He listened patiently while I explained that our immediate problem was to catch our breath, and that our party wasn't really dangerous because it stood for peace and order, without aiming at power. If any movement really deserved help, it was ours.

"With all the insults Jesus hurls at us!" Caiaphas exclaimed benevolently.

"Oratorical necessity," I replied.

"How about thirty thousand?" he said.

I was hugging myself with glee but hid it. "Well, if that's all you're ready to give." I said, feigning disappointment. I started to take my leave, but then brought out the second—the most important—part of my plan. I suggested that what would be most effective would be Jesus' arrest by the Temple guards. I hastened to explain that this would all be pretense, a maneuver that would benefit us both. By arresting and releasing Jesus, the Temple would assert its undisputed religious authority, and our party, by retiring in good order, would have shown it accepted it.

"Still subsidized," I said, to make things clear.

Caiaphas shook his head, laughing, and I was surprised to find my offer had not in the least surprised him.

"Please," I pressed him, humbly.

Back in Bethany, I told Jesus everything. It was settled! He turned pale, then seized me by the chest and shook me violently.

"Do you think," he breathed in my face, "do you think I've sunk to pretending I'm arrested?"

He was walking up and down, trembling, and happened to notice the letter of credit that had fallen on the floor. He picked it up, and tore it in half.

"I'd just like to say one thing," I said softly. "In politics there's only one thing that counts: success."

"And for us at the moment," I went on, "it's not a matter of success but a simple matter of survival. You all argue and talk, but without really knowing how much money is available. And I, who do know, say: take this chance."

He didn't speak. I wanted the choice to be his.

"What did he say to you?" he asked at last.

I repeated the whole episode.

"He was laughing, you know, but I could see that deep down he was worried. Oh, they're afraid of us all right."

"And is it quite certain," he said, in a grave voice, "that the whole thing would be kept between him and me?"

I had picked up the letter of credit and was joining the two pieces. "It'll still do," I said. We looked into each other's eyes.

So, keeping it secret from the executive, I went with Jesus to the Chief Priest to settle the affair. Caiaphas rose to meet us. He was small and frail. He gazed into Jesus' eyes with his little eyes, and, speaking formally yet kindly, asked him to sit down. He sent for something to drink and finally dealt with our business.

"My son, do you realize how many of you there are who want to free this country, some spiritually, some physically? There are the Heirs of Moses, the Movement for Freedom of the Spirit, Our Country, Our United Country, the Sentinels of Sinai, the current brand of neo-prophetism, the Essenes and the Zealots (and the Lord preserve us from *them*), the Middle Eastern League, the Philotheans (Heaven knows what they mean by that), the Voice of God, the Voice of Abraham, the Voice of Jacob and one called just The Voice. There's a movement that calls itself Redemption and another, which I heard of for the first time only yesterday, called Stop the Sun. You all want to do something, and your particular ambition is to be arrested. The Romans know you and turn a blind eye, leaving us in the Temple to settle things, although with this procurator, Pilate, they've grown more difficult. I believe in your sincerity, I believe your aim is noble, that you have no ambitions of power, that you are too idealistic and too disdainful to have them, but what, in practice, are you aiming for?"

He was looking lovingly at Jesus and Jesus was looking at him without a word. Caiaphas went on to explain that the political situation was ambiguous, that the country needing a breathing spell, that the only determining factor was the Romans. Who, if you considered them simply as administrators, weren't at all the worst possible governors. Our people had known worse.

"I remember," he said, gazing at a distant point, "when I was young myself, and when I was one of you. What dreams, what illusions I had! Now people hate me, as they always hate authority. They accuse me, me and my whole family, of playing the Romans' game, and they don't realize that by pretending to serve the Romans I'm playing ours. Not that it matters. Time will justify me. I know I haven't betrayed my country's cause. On the contrary, I feel I've served it, by helping these movements to go on, by giving them a little money to continue. Because remember, the worst thing in life is not to be able to advance an ideal."

He had risen again and came around the table, and, having sat down in a small armchair opposite that of Jesus, had taken his arms and was shaking them feebly. And he hummed, as if remembering from afar:

"Awake, my people, to liberation . . ."

But his voice broke, and I realized his feelings had overcome him. For some seconds he was silent, his small beard trembling, and looking up with tearstained eyes he repeated: "What illusions."

He recovered himself, and sitting down again in his position of authority asked:

"What do you want, then?"

As Jesus and I had agreed, I did the talking, and repeated the terms we had already settled on. The High Priest turned to him:

"So that's the agreement, then?"

Jesus lowered his head, without answering.

"As you wish," said Caiaphas. "I'll see that you are arrested in some unfrequented spot, because we must avoid being conspicuous. Only as many as are needed to spread the news should be there. The Mount of Olives, say. Do you know Jerusalem well? It's a sparsely peopled hill just outside the city, where the Romans never go. I've already made use of it, on other occasions."

We agreed on the date, the time, and the exact place of the arrest, which would be made by a troop of ten Temple guards, and he warned us not even to feign resistance, but just to make enough of a racket to attract the attention of the few houses around there. So as to be clearly seen, the troop would carry lanterns. After a week's preventive detention without interrogation, Jesus would be released by the Sanhedrin, on condition he went back to Galilee for at least a year. After that, we should see.

He looked at Jesus again:

"Agreed?"

Jesus spoke at last: "Agreed."

98

Caiaphas smiled approvingly. "You're no chatterer, but that's just as well. Say yes, yes, no, no, for the rest comes from the Devil."

So we took our leave, seen out by an unctuous official who had waited outside and whose face I later remembered. Days of waiting passed. Jesus disliked this play-acting, and would rather have been arrested seriously. But he joked about it. He said ironically to me:

"You can truly say you fixed the whole thing."

On the eve of his arrest I advised him to collect the executive for supper, in order to drop some dramatic hints to prepare them for what was to happen. He asked me if it wasn't better to reveal the plan outright. His ingenuousness astonished me, and I explained that his arrest was partly to assert his hold over the executive once and for all and to get the better of Philip's supporters.

So, on a warm May evening, we met in the upper room of an inn for what was to be, as it turned out, our last supper.

❈  ❈  ❈

Thanks to the money we had received I had managed easily to order a four-course meal. But the meeting took an unexpected turn. Clearly we were not the only ones who had acted in secret. The executive itself had done the same thing. Philip's supporters had won over the waverers and now formed the majority. Only Peter, John and Andrew had stayed out of the plot, still on our side. When the twelve of us, and Jesus, had sat down at table, the attack started at once. For the first time Philip proposed a motion of no confidence in the leader.

99

"We don't mean to throw you out of the executive," he said, looking bitterly at Jesus, "but to replace you as leader. The party has no money and no supporters. The authorities are watching us, and we're risking arrest at any moment. The least you can do is give up the leadership. I propose that at the end of supper the motion be put to the vote."

We began eating in silence. The food was good and the wine even better, which made the conversation flow. When we got to the fruit, as he wiped his mouth with his napkin Jesus gave me a meaningful look and banged his knife on the jug to get silence.

"You talk of a crisis in the party," he began, "and of the danger of arrest. But suppose I was the only one to be arrested, actually tomorrow, thus exonerating the lot of you?"

He seemed to me supremely sure of himself, as if the challenge of the opposition had stimulated and indeed exhilarated him. His opening remarks seemed to me very cunning.

"No one's going to arrest you on your own," said Philip pedantically. "We've made our inquiries. If it should happen, it would be all of us. And that's what we want to avoid, before it's too late."

"But suppose they arrested me alone," Jesus went on, skilfully, persuasively, "what would you say? If I were to tell you that when you drank that wine you were drinking my blood, what would you say?"

Philip slackened his belt and answered, with equal skill, although vulgarly: "I'd say it was excellent wine."

His followers all burst out laughing, and affected the others. Even Peter giggled a little.

Jesus, I saw, admitted the thrust had gone home.

"Yet a little while," he said coldly, "and I am not with you."

Everyone leaned forward to look at him, with the disappointment of a man interrupted during a meal. "What, off already?"

"He's going to be arrested, isn't he?" Philip exclaimed sarcastically. And, turning to Jesus: "You must have fixed things with the police, to be so sure. What arrogance you speak with!"

"I know more than you!" said Jesus, losing control and rapping the table with his knuckles.

"You always know more than the rest of us!" said Philip, raising his voice as well.

"Gently, gently," said Peter, trying to regain control. I saw that Jesus had turned pale and was making an effort to control himself. Staring straight ahead, he said resentfully:

"I always know more than you."

There was a murmur of protest, and I too disapproved of this outburst of pride.

"Frankly," said Philip, "some of the things you say ought to go into the minutes. I've a feeling you're taking yourself a bit too seriously."

"I am serious," Jesus answered, violently agitated.

"But we're all serious!" Philip exclaimed ironically. "And you've annoyed us with your great man's airs. No one's irreplaceable in a party, not even the leader."

Poisonously, he added: "Especially when he's an intellectual."

He had said what had long been gnawing at him, and all his supporters nodded vigorously, to back him. Yet, as I looked around at them all, I realized that the executive wasn't yet altogether united. They were leaning against the backs of their chairs, bellies full, idly following the argument that until now had been confined to Jesus and Philip. Two tramp musicians, one blind and the other crippled, came in at this point and were welcomed as an opportune interruption. They sang a couple of songs, went around with the plate, one guiding the other, and making salacious jokes, they left.

"And now for the motion," Jesus said sharply. "To the vote!"

Everyone was startled, at last. They had been surprised in a state of sleepy sensual well-being that makes "committed" men suddenly feel ashamed, deep inside. With an effort they looked at one another, while Jesus bit the corner of his lip. He was hating them all and hating himself even more because he hated them. It was at that moment that his intellectual pride got the upper hand over his political cunning, and he said with supreme intensity: "You don't know how much I love you. I'm not speaking figuratively. I love you. And that's why I'm ready to suffer for you."

"You flatter us," said Philip, bland and skeptical, "but this is hardly the right moment. Let's get on."

"Just a moment," said Peter, breathing heavily and looking at Jesus. "Just a moment. You said that in a little while you'd not be with us. Quite honestly I don't always understand you myself. What exactly did you mean? I'm speaking now as a party member who's worried about what's happening to the party."

"I mean to say that soon they'll arrest me."

"Oh, cut that!" exclaimed Philip.

"Will you let him explain!" cried Peter.

"He's pulling the wool over our eyes! He's always able to do that!"

"That's not true!" I shouted from my corner.

"You shut up!"

"You've always been jealous and you're jealous now!" I retorted. As I flung down these words, the whole table exploded like a volcano. Everyone was talking at once. Banging his fist on the wine-stained tablecloth Peter kept repeating:

"The party's got its statute and we must act according to that statute!"

Philip and Thaddeus were retorting with all the occasions on which Jesus had violated it. Andrew exclaimed:

"Dismissing the leader while the vote's being taken isn't in keeping with the spirit of the statute!"

"It is with the letter!" Thaddeus threw back at him.

For a moment Jesus covered his ears. That gesture quieted them all. In the strange silence that followed, Bartholomew, who never spoke, said:

"Wouldn't it be more reasonable to put off the discussion to another day, when we've cooled off?"

With a gesture, Thaddeus refused this and an uproar broke out again. Some of them had pushed aside their chairs and formed a group. Bunched together, their profiles almost touched. Then they went back to their places, to form other groups. Only Jesus stayed still. The argument was concentrated on a clause in the statute about the election of a leader. Apparently it wasn't clear. But the arguments used were phony and confused things still further. It seemed to me that in the confusion our hope of startling the executive by announcing Jesus' coming arrest was rapidly receding. I went around the table and murmured into his ear, suggesting we leave. He didn't answer. Philip noticed and hung on to my clothes.

"Here's someone who's going over to his side."

"Not me," I replied. "Because I'm with him already."

"In other words, you've been plotting behind our backs!"

The voices were all stilled. Through the open window came a scent of flowers from the garden below.

"Speak!" Peter said to Jesus.

For a long time before he started Jesus was silent, his eyes shut. He seemed to me already tired, disappointed, disgusted.

"You ask me where I'm going. I've told you: to pay for you. There's an odd distributive law that says a man who suffers suffers for others as well as himself. Chance has picked him to take up a certain amount of the suffering that afflicts the world, suffering that, if distributed rationally and impartially, others should bear as well. Without realizing it himself, and without others realizing it, such a man suffers for everyone. Only *I* shall be arrested. And I shall suffer for you."

"We don't understand," said Philip, emptying his glass.

Jesus went on, seeming worried: "We must presume that even the most brutal murderer who's condemned to death suffers on account of us, who call ourselves clean and innocent. His crime was committed through impulses we don't understand, impulses we might have shared, but in fact he alone felt. So when he pays for it, he suffers for us as well."

Philip was leaning back in his chair and gazing at the

ceiling. Thaddeus sniggered, picking his teeth with a fingernail.

"All right then," said Philip, "let's all start suffering, if that's the moral thing to do!"

"That's not it exactly," said John. "It's that . . ."

He looked about, unable to explain himself.

Peter said: "It means we're all executioners, that man's content to see his fellowmen suffering."

"It's not that either," said Bartholomew softly.

"Put it any way you like," said Philip, "the argument's irrelevant to what our party's out for."

"And just to get to the point," Thaddeus went on, with his heavy sarcasm, "show us how you're really suffering. Then I'll tell you I'm sorry, but sooner you than me! And that's the moral of life!"

"And a lousy one, too," John said.

"Listen to our hero!" cried Thaddeus. "And I'd like to know what you're doing. Carrying the wine mug for others, are you?"

"I'm *not* saying to him: sooner you than me. More likely say it to you, with that mug of yours!"

Thaddeus, who had drunk rather too much, flung himself at John.

"Stop it!" yelled Peter, rising. But the pair of them were already rolling on the floor, at the feet of Jesus. It was an appalling scene and, in parting them, Bartholomew got a scratch on the nose himself.

Thaddeus, who was stouter than John, shouted as the others held him back:

"Show me a man who carries others' burdens, and then I'll shut up!"

"I do," said Jesus, without moving.

"You? How, and where?"

"I'll do it."

"You'll do it!" Philip intervened, restoring order somewhat. "I'll do it too, inevitably, because sooner or later we've all got to suffer. I shan't spend my life sitting here!"

"So if I have the bellyache," said Thaddeus in his harsh voice, "is it to relieve someone who hasn't?"

Some of them laughed feebly. Peter shook his head.

"He means to say something more important than that. I think he means that there's suffering in the world but that some suffer and some don't. He's saying that we should all suffer equally. As it doesn't happen that way . . ."

Philip interrupted coldly: "I see we're going on with this abstract talk, so I recall the executive to the agenda. Let's get on with the voting."

The lamplight had grown dim, someone turned up the wick and a bright glow made our shadows enormous on the walls.

"And if we want to argue," Philip went on, to end the argument once and for all, "even if we want to argue about the suffering of the world, and its unfair distribution, we already know what's the most we can do: we can distribute what we *can* control fairly, that is, riches. In other words, social justice. Further than that we can't go."

"But when have we been simply socialists?" said Jesus softly. "If, when I'm gone, you make our movement into one for social justice, it will last a generation."

"There speaks the intellectual!" said Philip, excitedly. "Listen to the intellectual—far from the facts of life, from the people, from society!"

Jesus repeated, absorbed: "You still haven't understood, Philip, that man is social only in the lesser part of himself, and that the greater part of him is alone."

"Look what he's falling into—elitism, decadence, laissez-faire. Anyway, man is impotent!"

Here Philip changed the subject, but I must admit he made his point. He said that the theory of having to love our neighbor because he suffered unjustly didn't always hold water. There was one sort of "neighbor" whose sufferings, when they got their desserts, shouldn't arouse our pity: the wicked, the exploiters, the oppressors, the violent. All the atrocities that war criminals have perpetrated against our eternally persecuted people he set down before us; his outburst covered the whole range of passions and deserves to be recorded: "A man who rapes women before hanging them, who crushes children's heads for fun, who tortures, whips, beats and murders, who keeps you in a cage till you get as thin as a skeleton, who breaks your face up with his fist, who smashes your head against a wall, who beats your nose in, who drowns you in dung, who makes you die slowly by swinging you on a bar by your arms, who hangs your children up like paper decorations, grinning; must we love him if we see him suffer his punishment later? A man who, with his cronies, burns you alive, freezes you in icy water, keeps you on your knees for days, shut up in a dark cell for weeks, squashes you into a hovel after he's ripped out your nails, stuffs you with salted food to see if you die of thirst, whips you and then brings you around to see if he can go on whipping you, does experiments on your children and gives them plague and typhus, runs needles into your testicles and pokes red-hot rods into your wife's womb, flays your skin off to make lampshades, castrates you, starves you till you bite off the buttocks of your father's corpse, pins you under water to see how long you can hold out, puts lice in your filthy soup, makes you wear wooden clogs without stockings, you and your brothers, who can't be distinguished from your sisters and your wives, all tubercular, all with shaven heads and dead eyes, who makes your mother dash around naked to escape the gallows, makes you sleep with corpses and carry monstrous weights, and in the end nails you up on a stick. Must we love *him?*"

In the deep silence that followed, Jesus was silent. Then he replied:

"Yes, even him."

Philip turned over the table, yelling: "Betrayal!"

Some were shaking their heads, as if choking. Then they got up from their seats and wandered about the room, as if in a maze, two or three of them talking at once. Philip, Thaddeus and Simon had drawn apart, and were looking rancorously at the others.

"So," said Peter, turning to Jesus, and clearly disturbed, "what are we to make of your argument? Where's our party going? And what's this business about an arrest?"

Jesus answered: "You've already understood."

Philip ran behind him and yelled into his neck: "I have not understood."

Without turning Jesus repeated:

"You have understood."

"I'm not a murderer!" Philip was foaming at the mouth. "And I'm not prepared to console the man who persecutes me, and to suffer for him!"

"They will arrest me," Jesus went on, "and I will suffer for those who arrest me, and for everyone. What matters is for men to realize this injustice. Therefore I say to you, before I go: behave in such a way that, while men are happy, they will remember that at that moment others are suffering for them."

He took a piece of bread, and dipping it into the wine, held it out delicately to Philip, explaining that, in commemoration of him, we should do this: eat a piece of bread dipped in wine, thinking of the body and blood of all those who at that moment were suffering for us, because of the unfair distribution of suffering.

Disgusted, Philip said: "A stunt to trick us, as usual!"

"What you were drinking and enjoying until now was my blood," Jesus answered.

Philip flung away the sodden bread, poured out a chaliceful of wine and drank it. Then, with Thaddeus and Simon, he lumbered over to the door. But again he turned, pointed a finger at Jesus and said: "You've ruined the party, with your intellectuality!"

"Betrayer of the people!" Thaddeus cried.

They went out shouting: "Quitter! Coward!"

Peter ran after them, we heard exclamations, then he came back, looking down, and we had no idea what to do. What Jesus had said had won us over. For the first time we felt that he had, thanks to an intellectual effort, broken through the narrow confines of the world. At last we had understood that human pain can be understood, and God and our neighbor loved, only through the intellect. But where were we personally going to end? The party had broken up. Others would leave, after Philip. A future full of uncertainty and danger was opening up before us.

Would what Jesus said ever be understood?

I even thought no, because it was tainted from the start: this arrest, this sacrifice, this pain suffered "for others" was all a fraud.

Oh God, God! I took my head in my hands.

The scraping of our chairs as we got up sounded to me like the framework of a building crumbling; we went down the stairs one behind the other, and spread out under the stars. The others talked wearily as I paid the bill. We went our ways. Only Peter said softly to Jesus: "Till tomorrow."

When we were back at the hotel all I had to say to him was: "Well, you got your majority, anyway."

He gave me a smile that was like a grimace. When I said goodnight, he didn't answer. I peered at him through a crack in the door. He was sitting at the table, talking to himself.

❋   ❋   ❋

Next evening at sunset all of us, except Philip, Thaddeus and Simon, went to the Mount of Olives, as had been arranged. Jesus had tried to dress well, as if for a special occasion, but he was worried.

As it was the vigil of the feast, I had arranged for one of our agents to invite us to the garden of his small country house for a chat. It was a heavy evening, the sirocco was blowing, and the olive trees were shaking uneasily, as if with fever. In the light of the dying day, the ravines around Jerusalem seemed covered in a dark purple cloak.

Ephraim, the agent, was welcoming, and we settled in his garden looking at the clouds that were running low and red. It might rain. We spoke little, still worried by what had happened the previous evening. At one moment the conversation turned to a practical matter, the tactics to be followed in case of repression by the police.

"Escape and pretend not to know each other," Jesus said. "The party needs men to carry it on, not martyrs."

Peter observed softly: "But if we have to deny the party, then what does belonging to a party mean?"

Jesus answered impatiently: "A party's made up of living men, not of names carved on a memorial. What use are the dead? What's the point of sacrificing yourself?"

"Yet there's nothing like example to persuade and to draw people after you," said Peter. "Nothing can be achieved without personal sacrifice."

"Romanticism!" exclaimed Jesus, irritated.

"But isn't that the spirit of what you were saying at supper, yesterday evening?" John said humbly.

"No, it is not! The fact that a man suffers, and by suffering suffers for others as well, doesn't mean that he wants to suffer. We've got to avoid suffering, because it will come uninvited. We must hate suffering, drive it out. Or else we die."

And I heard him add darkly: "And no one wants to die."

We were all silent, oppressed by the hot air.

Ephraim brought more wine, which was drunk unwillingly. When Jesus went into the house I took the chance of following him.

"They should be here in half an hour," I told him.

"What annoys me," he said, at the door of the latrine, "is the people who'll come running to have a look."

"People are always won over by a good show," I said encouragingly.

He went into the latrine, and, dropping down suddenly on to a stool panted: "I don't like it. If only we could avoid this filthy display."

The small window banged in a gust of the sirocco and I remember how it hurt me to see him in that hovel, a poor boy strung between conscience and ambition. Looking at me with a smile, he went on:

"I will tell you. My weak point's always been decision. I've never been decisive in anything, anything!"

It was true. But he had understood, and spoken, sublime truths. He had discovered the roots of human suffering and the means of redeeming us from it. If we had put his words into practice our movement would have triumphed. He had shown us the way, the truth, the life. Wasn't that prize enough for him? Why did he want to assert himself personally in the world? And to assert himself on what? On those he praised for ideological reasons but in his heart despised? I felt that in him I was seeing the fate of all men of intellect. Touching him timidly on the shoulder I said, with enormous tenderness:

"The success you long for is the only thing that matters to me in life. Remember your Judas."

He pressed my hand gently, and sighed: "We're sure it will go well, aren't we?"

But someone was running towards us. He was looking for me. A man I didn't know, who looked like a servant, drew me aside and, scarcely able to speak with the effort he had made, told me the Chief Priest wanted to see me at once at his house. My heart sank. Without even telling the others I plunged after him down the slope, dragging my leg behind me; then dashed through the lanes sobbing and panting, and arrived at the High Priest's house in pieces.

"Where is he?" Caiaphas ran up to me, extremely agitated.

I dropped into a seat, unable to speak. The High Priest seemed to have gone mad.

"Run, run, run! Get away! Escape!"

I clutched at his clothes.

"A spy," he said hastily. "The Romans suspect a political plot between you and me. They're setting out to arrest Jesus themselves. Save him!"

Desperately I rushed to the door. Again I saw the face of that discreet official. Breathlessly I rushed back along the lanes, took a wrong turn and got lost in the lower city. It was now well into the night and no one was out of doors. I dashed about, sobbing with effort, banged on a couple of doors to ask the way, was told it, went wrong again, and ended crawling up a path that rose steeply to the vineyards. Realizing I was on a ridge at the back of the Mount of Olives I decided to carry on that way, as it was the shortest, even if the most difficult.

On my left I saw a line of lights climbing up the road, and recognized the Temple guard, obviously still not warned of what was happening.

I hurled myself up the steep hill, my heart bursting. Halfway up I saw another line of lights coming up on the other side. It was the Romans. I calculated that, by pushing on hard, I might reach the house before the two columns and give warning. On the plain where the olive trees grew the crumbly earth got into my boots and I pulled myself along from one tree trunk to the next. Every step was a nail that went deeper into my flesh.

113

Again I fell on my knees, and dragged myself along the ground. With a mist before my eyes I saw the two lines of lights climbing parallel with me, neither seeing the other, but both converging on the same point. I climbed up on a fallen tree trunk which had rolled into a ditch, and got over it, scratching my hands. The two columns were now quite near me. Already I could see the roof of the house, with dark clouds above it. I tried to shout. The first drops of warm rain fell, and I heard thunder in the distance.

The lanterns were nearby, tossed wildly by the sirocco. For the last time I hoisted myself up. I was level with the house. We saw one another now, the Temple guards, the Romans, and I. I hobbled forward.

"Jesus!"

I reached the gate at the same time as the Roman warrant officer commanding the troop. A straggling crowd had gathered. I shouted something in his face, and he shoved me aside. They all went in, dragging me along, crushed in that awful tramp and clanking of feet and iron.

"Jesus!"

I saw him appear, prepared. I saw him see the Romans. I saw him see me among them. And his face fell, while the others fled like shadows. Gathering what strength was left to me, I sprang towards him, and kissed his face desperately. "My son," I moaned, overwhelmed, "my son." They left me sobbing on the ground, and my weeping echoed like an ass' bray.

❋ ❋ ❋

I have written all this down on the eve of the execution of Jesus, condemned by the Romans for sedition and incitement to revolt; and I will give it to someone trust-worthy, to bear witness for me. The others found out about the money I received from the Temple, about the dealings I had with Caiaphas. I explained. But they don't believe me. They avoid me like a leper.

What should I do? Go on living to explain how what was pretense became reality, or take my own life at once to show that my pain is no pretense, and that I too suffered for others?

# PART THREE

The
Testimony
of
Thomas
called
Didymus

THE TESTIMONY OF THOMAS, CALLED DIDYMUS. I am writing this as I suffer from doubt, so that one day, when I read it again, I can see whether I was right or wrong. My comrades despise me because I do not believe what happened. Yet what reason have they for believing, except this same faith that makes me doubt? Is my faith irreligious because it doesn't agree with that of the majority? I remember the moment I was first bewildered by doubt.

We had reached Calvary, that stifling afternoon. Crushed and powerless, I looked at Jesus, who was waiting. His other friends had vanished, and all trace of Judas was lost (later he was found hanging from an apple tree). One Simon of Cyrene, who had carried the gibbet, that is the transverse bar of the cross, had dropped it at the foot of the pole already set up on the mound, and had stood aside wiping off the sweat. I saw Jesus go up to this poor rough fellow, take him by the shoulders, gaze deeply into his eyes, and embrace him. The man fell over, dazed, while Jesus, seized by two Roman soldiers, was laid upon the gibbet, on the ground.

But what had happened? His face had turned suddenly white, he was gazing about and struggling breathlessly.

He was a man who did not want to die.

I drew back, astonished, while the Romans piled up on top of him, holding him down. Two women from the Welfare Office, who had brought a jar of drugged wine, had rushed away down the hill. Others had not had the courage to come up to the top. The centurion in command of the troop said to me:

"What happened to him, all at once? He was quite calm."

I drew away even farther.

"Let him alone," the centurion ordered. The soldiers stood in a circle, watching him bound to the gibbet, his face streaming, purple. The officer came over to me and asked if I knew him. I did not reply.

"Do you know him?" he repeated, raising his voice, straddling before me. I nodded. He gestured to me to follow him. I had been a follower of Jesus for two years, fascinated by his supreme calm and his fantastic knowledge. Of us all, I had been the only one who had the courage to follow him up there, because I am a doctor. No miracle ever worried him. Prophet or magician? Saint or imposter? I had wondered for years. You had to know him to understand his fascination.

I saw him raise a corpse, cure a leper, heal an epileptic, straighten a cripple. He multiplied bread a thousandfold. He covered his eyes and sixty miles away a child falling into a gully stopped in mid-air. He looked at a faded flower and it blossomed again. He touched a bud and in an instant it flowered.

One evening he said: "It's dawn," and the sun rose behind us. He looked at the moon and it disappeared. He gazed at the stars and they began wheeling around. If there was a wind, he made it drop. If it was calm, he blew with his lips and made a gentle breeze.

One day he raised his hand, and the sky divided to show the Kingdom of God. There was a light that in the center became golden, and in that circle appeared the face of a man in which each one of us recognized himself. It was then that he said:

"The light shineth in darkness; and the darkness comprehended it not."

Another day he became so small he passed through the eye of a needle, and so large that we could no longer see him. He stroked a dog and turned it into a lion, and the lion licked his hand.

He walked on the waters; he went into fire; he lived for two months without eating; he stopped breathing for hours. He stuck a knife into his heart and the smell of violets came from it. He could turn his face and become stone. He could be in several places at once and vanish

121

altogether. He shouted in Jerusalem and was heard at Beersheba. He passed through walls, he had eyes of fire, and at his smile the fields bloomed. I saw him lower his eyelids, and night fell as he did so. He could make it rain without clouds and the sun shine at two poonts in the sky.

He cut off a finger, planted it in a pot of earth, and made it grow till it put out another self that returned into him.

He could speak with the voice of a man and a woman, roar like a lion, rustle like petals closing, rumble like thunder, and send out a whole orchestra of sounds from himself. He could speak and write backwards and see in the dark.

He gave back youth to a white-haired old man and turned coal into gold. When he spoke before parchment his words were written on it.

He was magnetic. He drew down the sun and when people complained of the heat he ordered rain at once. He sent the sun away and when people complained of the cold he ordered the earth to generate heat. He made flowers grow up from ice. One night he made all the stars come closer and creation looked like an immense diamond, in which each one of us was an atom.

He carried us through space and we heard sounds we had never known, saw lights we had never seen, breathed an exhilarating air. When we returned to earth he sliced the globe in half and in its center he showed us that same man's face in which each one of us recognized himself.

He was a magician. But unlike so many others, what he gave was truth. What was truth? He often told us, but we did not understand:

€122

"I am truth."

He meant man.

So the Romans condemned him to death. But I, who saw him perform the final miracle, suffer and wonder: was he the truth, or was he an illusion? After all, he had performed miracles to show us that man's salvation could not come from the outside. Man must save himself. His miracles were a lesson, to make us mistrust them.

"Everything," he kept saying, "depends on man."

Earthly problems could be solved only through man's conscience, and miracles were just illusory solutions put forward by a wavering conscience.

"Be just what you are."

So he despised those who tried to solve matters of fact, like the freedom of the country, the distribution of wealth, the observance of rites. His approach was diametrically opposed to this. He would say:

"You will be free if you give up freedom, rich if you give up riches, devout if you give up devotions."

In the Temple they called him a heretic. He smiled, and performed another miracle. They did not understand and they thought he used this means to confound his critics and make himself recognized as the undisputed Messiah. There were riots. The Romans stepped in.

But now, facing the supreme sacrifice, why did he deny his teaching, why did he not want to die, why did he thrash so, straining at the ropes; he who had persuaded us to accept everything?

❅　❅　❅

"I want to know what happened to him suddenly," the centurion said impatiently. "Speak to him."

I leaned over Jesus.

"Master . . ."

He was thrashing more than ever. I was appalled.

The Romans gazed calmly at him, and gave a silent order. They stripped Jesus to the groin and a soldier began whipping him. When they had weakened him they held him still, and I heard the first blow, together with a scream. Then there was silence. I heard the clink of metal, curt orders, more blows. Already the soldiers were raising the gibbet, holding Jesus up by his feet. They laid it against the pole and hammered in the last nails. It was now a cross. The women with the drugged wine came forward. It was too late—I shook my head.

The soldiers had moved away and were eating.

"Did you know him?" the centurion asked me, biting into a roll. I nodded. "Is it true he did miracles?"

I hung my head, without answering.

"But he couldn't do the final one!" the centurion grinned.

At that moment I saw Simon getting up again, like a man awakened from sleep. He gave a suspicious glance at the cross.

"Wait, you!" I called.

He quickened his heavy pace.

I caught up with him. "When you met the Roman troop that ordered you to carry the gibbet," I said, "what was the condemned man like?"

"Scared, trembling."

"That's not true. I saw him myself."

"Then why ask me?"

He started downhill again, his huge body shaking. I

frowned. What had really happened? The Romans were playing dice, the centurion was yawning with boredom, it grew hotter and hotter. Lower down the hill the onlookers stood about: a pervert, two women, an idiot talking to himself, two small boys who later ran off incredulously, three peasants who happened to be passing, a witch hoping to get some of the blood for her disgusting spells.

Jesus opened his mouth, and a raucous sound came from it. I pointed to the glass of wine. One of the guards stood on a stone and lifted it. The liquid spilled on his chest. The pervert's lips opened greedily. I heard Jesus gurgling disconnected words. The flies were already going into his throat. He began spitting them out. Insects swarmed into his wounds. One of the women suggested:

"Couldn't he be fanned?"

"Get back," the centurion yelled.

I had had a chance to watch crucifixions before and knew what this form of torture was. It was not pain, loss of blood, fever, hunger, thirst, cold or heat that brought on death. It was slow suffocation. I had tried it myself, by hanging by my arms on a bar. In a few minutes you cannot breathe, the muscles are paralyzed and block the lungs. The flesh of his arms was swelling up into lumps, which contracted until his whole body was heaved up. This allowed him to open his lungs, but then he would fall back again and we heard the hiss of his choking trachea.

After an hour he had scarcely weakened at all. I knew it would take three hours at least; wretches given a seat to support them lasted for days. To the centurion, I suggested breaking his shinbones to deprive him of support and

125

speed up suffocation. But the centurion stood quite still, arms crossed.

"There's a plum tree in Sannio, with its fruit already ripe, fine, smooth, bluish, like the nipples of Lybian negresses. Pick them in the dark and swirl them around in your mouth, like this."

From the cross came a bestial howl.

"And soon there'll be the grapes, lovely, swollen, sweet."

Clouds had massed and hung over us like globes of fire. The two small boys had come back with others, and were staring silently. Distant thunder was heard. His thorax was blown out like a lobster pot, and at the navel his belly was hollow. Sweat was pouring off him. It was clear, from the way he gazed, that he was still conscious. In his eyes I seemed to read: You don't know what you're doing. Had he understood and accepted himself now, when it was too late? I shall always remember that light from his eyes, the mildest I had ever seen.

His body was now black with flies. He lifted himself up so high that we heard a tearing sound. The nails had ripped right through both feet and they oozed like meat hung up at the butcher's. His belly had become a ball, his thorax closed up, like paper. This lasted a few seconds and then he fell again, his chest smashed like a birdcage.

I thought that, unsupported, he would very soon choke. And in fact the hissing started again, each hiss growing longer. The small crowd grew hysterical.

"Lance him!" they shouted.

"That's enough!"

Even the flies had flown off him, and buzzed wildly in circles.

"Now he'll fall off," the centurion cursed.

"He won't," I said. "The nails in his wrists are resting on transverse bones. You're experts without knowing it."

It was no longer sweat that was flowing from him. It was his whole life. His body was emptying like a squeezed sponge. He hung stiff, gleaming. A deafening thunderclap burst out.

"But why isn't he finished yet?" the Roman shouted to me in the rain. People ran down the hill, while the soldiers pulled their cloaks over their heads and Simon crouched there, rock-like.

"It's not easy to die," I shouted. "If it was, what would be the point of martyrdom?"

Now that the rain had washed him the symmetry of Jesus was perfect. There was no difference between his body and the wooden post. The storm passed, the Romans came out from their cloaks, the mound was veined with filthy rivulets. In the sudden coolness something shot down from above. A white eagle was perched on the cross and was glaring at us with its terrible stern eyes and feathers like marble.

"Get it!" the centurion shouted greedily.

They flung lances at it, and tried to cut off its head with dagger blows. Like the heavens opening, the eagle rose and vanished.

Simon had come up to us.

"What do you want?" the centurion cried angrily.

"He's dead," I said.

We went over to the cross. A soldier pulled him by the feet. He was as hard as a dried fish.

"It took long enough," sighed the centurion. He nodded to the soldier, who plunged his lance in his heart. Reddish water flowed out.

"That's it," said the centurion, satisfied. "Anyone want him?"

❋    ❋    ❋

"If you want it," said Simon, "I've got a tomb."

But Peter, John and four others were already running over. When they saw me they looked apologetic, the way people do when they have been cowardly. But I felt kindly towards them. I spoke to the centurion.

"Got the license?" he asked.

I took it out. "Right," he said.

They were moving off, drying out their clothes on their lances, and seen from behind they looked like purple crows. We lowered the gibbet to the ground, unnailed the wrists and folded the arms. And so we took him down, carrying him like a plank through the few who stood stiffly there, without speaking. I turned. Simon was following us.

"Anything else you want?"

"The gibbet," he said, "belongs by right to whoever carried it up."

"Then take it," I told him.

He pointed out that this was impossible. John had it on his back.

"But it doesn't matter," he said. "If you want it for the funeral, I'll come along and collect it later."

He looked at me slyly and said "Where will it be?"

"Near here, in the garden of a man called Joseph."

"Ah," he said shaking his head, very much the knowing peasant, "Joseph of Arimathea. I know him."

He came closer to me and said carefully, so that I should not fail to understand: "Then I'll collect the gibbet there."

I found him loathsome. I said "All right."

"And when is the funeral?"

He noticed how indignant I was, and put forward his hands. "Don't worry, we've agreed."

"Tomorrow!"

He withdrew, repeating obsequiously: "Tomorrow. I'll come and fetch it the day after tomorrow, then. You do realize, sir," and he raised his voice rather resentfully, "that even a bit of timber's worth something to a poor peasant."

This time it was I who went over to the creature, forgetting the others who, bending over, were walking fast down the hill.

"You'd eat a dead man's liver," I told him.

He grinned: "It all goes to make soup."

He warded off my hand and went on, sardonically but cruelly: "We're all of us condemned, sir. What's the difference between the man on the cross and the man who's still below? We may use a lot of fine talk but in practice, what do we do? If you'll excuse my saying so, sir, I don't believe in anything, and when it's my turn, that's that."

I disliked his cynical servility and as the runaway group grew smaller below us I wanted to explain that what mattered wasn't death but its pain. To my amazement he read this in my eyes and said: "You're right, sir, but the pain of death is part of the pact."

I looked at him, startled. "What pact?"

"The pact of life. Sir, let me ask you this: Why do you pity the man who was condemned? We're all condemned. And then death in itself doesn't mean suffering. If you'll allow me to say so it's not suffering that counts. It's the unknown we're worried about. Man is afraid to die, but he doesn't really know why."

Lowering his voice and towering over me, he said scornfully: "Everyone feathers his own nest, and I feather mine. You delude yourself you're caring for others by pitying their pain. But the fact is you and others like you are all feathering your own nests as well. There's no such thing as altruism. There's no such thing as love. There's no such thing as anything except us, who are longing to live. Do you know what I say, sir? You all disgust me. Give me a drink any day, rather than your sort of charity."

I was raging, confused.

"Goodnight," he said, mocking me. "I'll come and get the gibbet the day after tomorrow."

I started to join the others. After a step or two I turned back. He had vanished.

❋ ❋ ❋

From here I will present the facts like a news story, relying on what others said and what I saw myself, and again I wonder: Who can blame me for being incredulous? Isn't faith a constant struggle against doubt?

The burial took place as we had arranged. When we had carried the corpse to the sepulcher, a small natural cave behind a hill surrounded by clumps of low trees, we washed it with aromatic water, then Mary and Magdalen rubbed it with scented oils. We wrapped the wounds in cloth soaked in aloes and myrrh, and put the body in the hollow, laying it on the colored mosaic. We had dressed him in a garment of white linen, and he was stiff, unreal, as if he had never lived. In order to give our souls some sense of purpose, we felt, rather strangely, that we must keep busy, and insisted on giving the body all the finishing touches.

Peter gathered us together, we quickly said a prayer, then, one by one, we went out of the tomb. Three of us pushed the great stone into the opening and then each of us went home on his own. It was arranged that we would not be seen together in Jerusalem and would meet at the grave the following morning to celebrate the rites. Night was falling.

The first definite fact is that Magdalen, having returned to the tomb next morning at five, found a gardener there. This man was trying to move the great stone by himself, but when he saw her he stopped and pretended to be saying a prayer. Obviously the gardener, who was Simon of Cyrene, had thought it too early for any of the dead man's family to be there.

"What are you doing here?" Magdalen asked him, as she herself told me three hours later.

The man muttered something, in a way that seemed to her suspicious, and left, once looking back over his shoulder. When I heard this I went to look for him at once, but could not find him. We conducted the funeral rite by laying the gibbet under Jesus' neck to remind ourselves of his martyrdom, and left the sepulcher, meaning to come back on the next three days, as is our custom.

But I knew what I was going to do in the meantime. When night fell I settled down behind the sepulcher, and soon afterwards heard cautious footsteps. Even before peering into the darkness, I guessed who it was.

"Already?" I said, looming up in front of him. He leapt back in alarm.

"Who is it?"

"You know who it is," I replied. "What do you want here, at this time of night?"

His voice sounded sullen and impatient: "The gibbet."

"Didn't we agree you were to come tomorrow?"

He raised his voice: "Where is it?"

"And what were you doing here this morning, at dawn?"

He moved as if to push me off with his powerful arm, and grunted:

"Get out."

I was afraid of the darkness and of that strange presence. And when he glared at me and I saw his eyes glittering like coals, I shrank back. The man sniggered, and slouched backwards.

"Right, as we agreed. I'll come tomorrow. But someone might take it away, if you leave it unguarded—you must see that."

"Take what?" I said, trembling.

Having realized what I meant, he did not answer right away. Then he said scornfully:

"The beam, of course. If you really must know, it'll do me for the roof, and if I had to buy it that would be at least ten denarii."

"Take it, I took it out on purpose; it's leaning against the rock behind the tomb."

"Oh no," he said, withdrawing still farther away, "there's no hurry. Now that I know, I shan't worry."

Still he hung about, a bulky shadow. But it was no longer he who was weighing on me, it was the enormity of my doubt. I hurled myself on him, trying to shake him.

"You dirty dog, you were trying to get into the tomb this

morning. What were you up to? Tell me!"

He made no movement and removed me like a feather. Then he muttered, with an injured air:

"Don't hurt a poor peasant, sir. I was afraid the gibbet had been forgotten inside. Excuse me, sir, but I've got to go and water my animals."

I saw him move heavily away, under the stars; and I leaned against the great stone, trying to move it to make sure the body of Jesus was still inside. Exhausted, I fell to the ground, while an owl whistled. I went home troubled and flung myself on the bed without even undressing.

It was three in the morning when I awoke with a start. Without even thinking of what I was doing, I dashed out. I remember the Pleiades leaped before me, strung to a crescent moon, while the sky rolled around. I had to press my eyes hard to stop it doing so, and rushed out of the town. Like a dog pursued I ran fast and when I reached the sepulcher flung myself on the ground panting. The sky was rolling around again and I turned over on to my back and made myself stare at it. Then I got up and approached the tomb, trembling. At that moment I felt the same shock that had aroused me from sleep. It was open.

I stood quite still in front of the opening without the courage to go in. Then I entered. It was empty. I touched the walls and the mosaic, to reassure myself that there was no mistake. It was empty. In the cave's opening the sickle moon looked to me like an enormous laugh.

Under the stars I hurled myself towards a point in the countryside where Simon had his hovel. Twice I fell over, and ended up in a newly-scythed field, where, in the shivering dawn, I caught a glimpse of something dark. It was his hut. A flock of ducks was flying over as I reached it, and I saw a stork standing straight on one leg at about the point where the sun would be rising. A dog came at me, barking, and right afterwards a woman's head popped out.

"Where's Simon?" I asked.

"Where is he?" she repeated shrilly.

"Where's Simon?" I repeated, more loudly.

"Where is he? Where is he?" the woman started shrieking.

She told me he had not been home for two days and that the last time they had seen him he was carrying a gibbet on his back, for a man the Romans were to crucify.

"And didn't he come home that evening?"

He had not only failed to come home, the woman told me, growing progressively shriller, but no one had seen him again.

"Well I have," I said. "More than once, and only a few hours ago."

"Where is he? Where is he?" the woman started shouting again.

I told her I wanted to talk to him on business, and asked her if, in the last few days, Simon had been looking for timber to repair the roof. With her head stuck out of the window she looked at me, without understanding. Then she came out barefoot, while the dog, tied on a rope, crouched in his hole.

Abruptly, I asked her: "What sort of a man is your husband?"

"He's not my husband!" she replied.

"What sort of a man is he?"

Oh, a fine man, the woman said, as if reciting a litany,

holy and devout, a man who lived for nothing but his work and who helped the poor.

"And we're poor enough ourselves," she added, whining.

She wrinkled up her small eyes, and coming right up to me, in order to see me better, said: "You've come about the taxes, haven't you?"

"No."

She turned away and pretended to be busy, calling the dog, the chickens, the goat. "We don't owe anyone anything," she explained, settling herself before me, her toes splayed out on the ground. "We're respectable. Where's Simon?"

I left without answering. From a distance I could still hear her yapping after me, her shrill voice disturbing the quiet of the dawn. I went and woke Peter and told him what had happened.

When we rushed to the sepulcher it was already day. A hundred yards from it Magdalen appeared; she had arrived before us and was fleeing in terror. Peter covered her mouth with his hand, and peering about we cautiously approached the small cave, surrounding it. The great silence was broken only by a rustling of trees. Scents were wafted from the opening of the tomb. They came from the cloths left on the floor.

"He is risen!" Magdalen burst into sobs, covering her face with her hands and falling on her knees.

"Ssh!" said Peter angrily. She was groaning. Peter exclaimed: "Can it really have happened the way he told us: 'I will rise again'?"

My mind filled with thoughts, I was silent.

"Or do you think the Temple people took him? They're capable of anything, filthy swine that they are, God curse them all. Filthy, stinking swine, lousy cowards, may God . . ."

He was wandering about, holding his head.

"He is risen," the girl repeated ecstatically. "He is risen."

The birds had started singing, and when the sun rose its rays made the rock gold and reached inside the sepulcher, making the mosaic glitter.

"Oh!" Peter could not bear his own tension, and fell on his knees as well, adoring. I was the only one left standing and could not tear my eyes away from the cave. Quickly I thought: "Obviously Simon came during the night, removed the stone and took away everything, gibbet and corpse. It's clear he'd already tried twice, and been interrupted first by Magdalen, then by me. But where is Simon now?"

"Yes," shouted Peter, as if he had suddenly discovered something. "It's true! He is risen!"

He spoke excitedly, as if he wanted to convince himself more than others. "How many times did he tell us! And only the other day he said it again: 'I came into the world from the Father; now I am leaving the world to return to the Father.' After all the miracles he did, it was natural he should do this one!"

He looked at me, standing silently, and shouted desperately: "It is so!"

"I don't know."

"What do you mean, you don't know?" He grabbed at my chest.

"If he wanted to do another miracle," I said, freeing myself, "why didn't he escape before they put him on the cross?"

"To show he was immortal!" Peter said, obstinately.

"To teach us," Magdalen added.

"You don't believe it," Peter grabbed me again.

"Let me alone!"

We were circling around each other, and once more Peter burst out against the Temple people. Then he fell on his knees, saying he was convinced that Jesus had risen.

"You won't believe it because you're a doctor!" he cried, tugging my clothes. "But it's true! My faith's greater than your science!"

I flew into a rage: "My faith's as good as yours!"

"Then believe it!" He tugged me so hard that I fell over. He stood over me, shaking my shoulders like a wrestler. "Believe it, if you really have faith!"

When he saw I had no intention of fighting he straightened up, helping me and trying to get his thoughts in order, and as he did so, picking up the grave-clothes. Then he became frightened, and, guessing that the authorities would accuse us of having robbed it, he decided that the best thing to do was shut the sepulcher up again, keep quiet and wait.

"You're talking logically at last," I said.

We hurried back to Jerusalem, having arranged to meet secretly that same evening, at Luke's house. But I lost no time, and took advantage of my visits to patients to start collecting information about Simon right away.

"Ah yes," said an asthmatic old man, "the chap from Cyrene. He wasn't even born in Cyrene, as it happens. His father was. He had a farm down there."

From a bedridden old woman I heard that he had left his wife and was living with another woman. "Who's made a slave of him!" she added, waving her hand. From a married couple I learned that Simon was a good fellow who never drank and hardly ever spoke to a soul. A peasant, on the other hand, told me he had been a sailor and had a past; and a woman I had helped in childbirth the previous week said that he was a heavy drinker, and lazy.

"We were in the army together," a gardener the same age as Simon told me. "Then we each went our own ways. He's a good, steady man."

"That thief!" said a craftsman whose teeth I was treating. "He still owes me for a pair of sandals I sold him a couple of years back."

"That nice man who always brings us the first fruits!" exclaimed a rich landowner's wife.

I was surprised how hard it was to form a picture of someone on the basis of what those who knew him said. I went back to the hut.

"If it's about the taxes," said the woman aggressively, "we're too poor."

"I'm a doctor, not a tax collector. Is Simon ill at all?"

As she did not believe me, she gave no answer. I repeated the question. "He has his ups and downs, like everyone else. He gets diarrhea. And so do I. Now that you're here, you may as well examine me!"

She had dropped her dress off and was lying on the kitchen table, twisted as an olive trunk. I pretended to examine her and suddenly asked if they had quarrelled lately. She flung her legs down into her dress and pulled it up.

"If it's because he's dead and you want to know if he

made a will, then no, he didn't make one! In any case, his stuff's mine already!"

Evening was falling as I walked home and the countryside was loud with frogs. I flung myself on the bed, my face deep in the pillow. Never in my whole life had I been so tired and empty. When I woke again the night's silence was buzzing in my ears and although it was late I went along to Luke's.

From the care with which the door was opened a crack, and the suspicious gleam of an eye, I realized something remarkable had happened. Magdalen opened the door, while Luke peered out quickly and shut it again. I went into the main room. Everyone there (about ten of them) was as silent as a statue. They seemed thunderstruck. When he saw me, Peter opened his mouth like a speaking corpse:

"He came to see us," he said.

I looked at each of them, one by one.

"Yes," said Peter, in what seemed to me an absurdly silly way, "he came. He asked us for something to eat. He ate."

"But who are you talking about?" I asked.

"Now you can't doubt any longer," he said. "It was he, in flesh and blood, who came while we were here together and said: 'Peace be with you.' We touched him, he asked us to, he was flesh and blood, it was him. He had the wounds of the nails in his wrists and feet."

"Did you," I asked automatically, "see the wound in his side as well?"

Peter's eyes flashed. Dropping down on a stool near the door, I repeated exhaustedly: "Did you see the wound in his side as well? And were the wounds in his wrists and feet real wounds?"

"Thomas, your incredulity's blasphemous!" Peter exclaimed.

"But it's important," I shouted back. I was holding my face in my hands and it was then I realized I was not going to be understood. I left.

That night I had restless dreams and when I woke at three in the morning I could not resist the temptation to go back to the empty sepulcher. I crawled along the ground to it, while the owl hooted. A cool breeze moved the leaves of the trees and the blood-red sickle moon was declining. The stars had faded. I felt defeated, desolate, and impotent.

"Oh Lord, Lord," I prayed, brow on the ground, "take away my incredulity, don't make me keep on suffering."

I slept without feeling the cold, and dawn woke me with a stray dog sniffing my neck. We looked into each other's eyes and he trotted away.

When I got home I had a hot bath, changed, ate a hearty meal and decided to face the problem logically, by telling my comrades what I knew.

❊  ❊  ❊

I began with Peter, whom I went to see at Luke's, where he was lodging. When I had told him what had happened from the time of the crucifixion till the present, I said: "Now you'll see why I was incredulous."

He shrugged as if he wanted to repudiate what I was saying before hearing it. Then he said, as if out of duty: "Which means?"

I paused a moment, then replied:

"Jesus never died."

Peter got up, knocking over the chair, and started to walk nervously around the table. "Leave us alone!" he shouted at Magdalen, who looked inside.

"Jesus performed his last miracle before the cross. He made a change of appearances between himself and Simon, when he embraced him, so it was Simon who was nailed up, Simon looking like Jesus, while Jesus stayed there watching what happened, looking like Simon."

Peter burst out laughing hysterically, pushing me away with one hand.

"So," I concluded in a hurry, "the man who looked like Simon but was in fact Jesus insisted on recovering the crossbar of the gibbet. Actually he wanted to get into the sepulcher to take on his own appearance and make the corpse vanish. As in fact he did."

"Come in!" Peter had flung open the door and called the others. John, Luke, Magdalen, another woman called Mary, and Matthew came in. Peter repeated my story, using a tone of voice that made it seem absurd. Two or three of them turned their backs on me, uneasily. Magdalen was staring at me strangely.

"The Master came here in person to see us, with the wounds of the nails, and he dares to make up a story like this!" said Peter mockingly.

Then he added:

"What can I say to you? You've been with us all this time and I still want to think of you as one of us, but what can we do with someone who thinks this way?"

I hung my head and answered: "Nothing."

*  *  *

Desperately I went on searching for Simon of Cyrene, without finding him. The hag had told the police about his disappearance, and made suspicious by my efforts to find him, they came and questioned me.

I said I had tried to get in touch with him to give him the gibbet he had asked for.

But the news got around. "Now you'll get us all involved," the others reproached me.

The police did in fact raid Luke's house. They asked general questions, opened cupboards, searched attic and cellar.

"Now you've stirred up the authorities," they said accusingly. "Please keep to yourself."

Three evenings later I was undressing for bed when a boy came and knocked cautiously at my door. He whispered that I must go to Luke's house at once. Peter himself opened the spyhole and then the door, laying a finger on his lips and puffing his cheeks out exaggeratedly. He listened outside for a moment and then, leaving another two on guard, led me upstairs. When I went in, either because the lamp was burning very brightly, or else for some other reason, I felt blinded and at first failed to recognize him. When I heard him call me "Thomas," I felt as if I were paralyzed.

I, who had seen him dead, nailed up, saw him alive again and smiling, finishing a meal. We looked into each other's eyes and Jesus saw that mine were full of doubt.

"Don't you yet believe that it is I resurrected?" he said, pouring himself some wine. "I got them to send for you on purpose, so you'd be convinced."

I bent my head, while the others watched, lined up against the walls.

"Yes," I said, recovering myself. "I believe you, more than ever."

"Perhaps," he said, "you'd like to examine me, to be sure?"

Suddenly he had uncovered his wrists and I saw two terrible, clear black holes. He held out his feet, wearing shoes, and I saw the same sort of hole. He bared his ribcage, making everyone there shiver: between the fourth and fifth ribs there was a deep black incision.

I went up to him.

"You don't mind, do you?"

I put my finger into the holes in his wrists, touching them and trying out their articulation, which was perfect. How could this be? Of necessity the nailing must have broken the ulna and the scaphoid, at least. I pressed the flesh: it was not swollen. Indeed it was soft, and, apart from those two horrible holes, rosy. I knelt down and examined his feet—their articulation was also in order—and then his side. Here it was interesting to see how the point of the lance had gone in without tearing the flesh, but cutting it perfectly. These wounds looked unreal as if transferred from a body that had actually suffered them to another, on which they had been laid.

I straighted up, and looked at him.

"It is I," Jesus said gently, "come back to this world to show you that I am the resurrection and the life, and that whoever believes in me, though he die, shall live."

I asked: "Will you be staying long?"

He shook his head, meaning that he would be leaving forever.

I should have liked to say, sarcastically, you couldn't keep this pretense up indefinitely.

"Do you remember that poor peasant who carried the gibbet?" I asked him.

He nodded.

"He's disappeared," I went on They all held their breath, their faces so still that they seemed like pieces of stone hung on the wall.

I repeated: "He's disappeared. But you may know where he is."

He replied: "If anyone wishes to come with me, let him deny himself, take up his cross and follow me. He who seeks his life shall lose it, and he who loses his life for love of me, shall find it."

Like a man who has finally found out the truth, I took a deep breath.

"So it's true!" I said triumphantly. "Simon died in your place!"

"You swine!" Peter could no longer hold out and seized my shoulders. Uproar broke out, suppressed by fear of making noise. Through the arms that were pushing me out I caught a glimpse of Jesus' eyes watching me, while the others hissed:

"Traitor!"

"You were never one of us!"

Heavy blows fell on my back, and when I hit my head on the doorpost, they stopped. Peter was biting his fingers, regretting it.

"Don't worry," I said, embracing him. "I know it's not my doubts that trouble you, but your own, because there's no such thing as perfect faith."

I went back to Jesus, and, leaning my elbow on the table, gazed at him, studying him.

"I believe in you," I said in a firm voice, "but show me

that you're really dead. Show me that in order to conquer the Kingdom of Heaven life must really be renounced. Show me that all this isn't a play on words to hide the fact that the Kingdom of Heaven's already here on earth, and that that's why we cling so hard to life."

He had let me speak, and then, folding his napkin, replied:

"He who believes in me, believes not in me, but in Him who sent me."

"Then it's true that you personally don't matter," I cried. "That you personally may be like all the rest!"

He said: "I, the Light, came into the world so that whoever believes in me will not stay in darkness."

"Imposter!" I shouted in his face. "You're playing with words, the way you've always done."

Coldly he replied: "I say nothing of myself. The Father who sent me told me what I must say. The things I say, I say exactly as my Father told them to me."

"And who is the Father?" I said furiously, moving away from the table. "Is he just yours or is he everyone's? Why shouldn't we think you're a man like us, and that for that reason there's just one thing you want—to live on this earth, as in fact you're doing now?"

Bending over across the table, I seized him by the chest and shook him. "You never died! Another man died for you! Another man suffered for you! And now you come here to eat!"

Jesus got up and we all stood still. A strange light flowed from him, as if he were luminous within, and suddenly we found ourselves up in the sky, with his figure standing out distinctly against the sun.

He told us, "It is better for you that I go. Because if I do

145

not go the Comforter will not come. But if I go, I will send him to you."

He raised his hands and all the stars started whirling round his head, forming a crown. Then he moved away into the sun, leaving us, faint in the darkness. When we opened our eyes again, the lamp was out. It was I who got up to relight it. I saw Peter staggering and helped him to his feet. We looked at the rest on the floor, our legs trembling.

"Another miracle," I panted.

They got down on their knees and were softly chanting a prayer, while I wondered: What about Simon?

❖ ❖ ❖

We felt we must make a final on-the-spot investigation and when we had slept as best we could at Luke's house, we all went to the sepulcher. It was a mother-of-pearl dawn. The small leaves trembled coolly and tiny flowers poked through them like June bug wings. When the sun rose the universe looked like a block of gold and diamonds. Without speaking we pushed away the great stone. There was a sudden uproar. Four lances shot out of the tomb, while other Roman legionaries leaped on us from behind. Stupidly, we had fallen into their ambush, and we looked around like rats in a trap.

For ten days we were kept in separate cells and interrogated by a senior officer. Peter was beaten and Andrew hung upside down for over two hours. Magdalen had freezing water poured down her back, and, as I was a doctor, I was treated rather more delicately: they interrogated me for two days on end, till I lost consciousness and collapsed.

Having failed to get satisfaction, they brought us together and asked:

"Where's the corpse?"

Nobody answered. The chief of the military police spoke patiently: "We don't want to take it away from you. We don't collect corpses. Only, where is it?"

In the name of us all Peter answered: "Before he was crucified he told us: 'I am going where you cannot come.' Now, where is it we can't go? Up there. Which means he's risen."

The police chief sighed again and said, as if speaking to children: "And do you really think the procurator will accept an explanation like that?"

"Yes," answered Peter.

He went out and after an hour he came back. To our surprise he told us we were free, but that all must return to Galilee, except for Luke and me, who came from Jerusalem. In the hall of the fortress a tall officer, with an eagle eye and a long red cloak hanging from his shoulders, came towards us, looking inquisitive. He was a Jew like us, who collaborated with the Romans, and we afterwards learned he was called Paul of Tarsus.

"You're very odd people," he said, with a younger officer standing behind him. "Yours is probably the most devout religious sect in this country, and as a functionary of the political office I know you. You're not violent, and you're not even agitators, but what's your program? Is it the personality of the leader, who no longer exists? We can't find danger in you, so we're letting you go home. But what

I can't understand is this: how, without a program, without an organization, and without funds, without even a name, you're so devout and close-knit. I'm very curious about you."

He gave us a small, friendly smile that flickered out at once between the jaws shaved Roman-fashion, and went away, leaving an impression of strength and elegance. So much so that, in spite of the torture we had borne, we still spoke well of him.

I continued to make inquiries about Simon of Cyrene, who was now given up for lost, and occasionally saw Luke. One day I was going to Emmaus to see a rich patient recovering in the hillside town when a stranger popped out from the hedge and greeted me. Then he walked along with me. He was tallish, about thirty, wearing dark clothes and an odd wide-brimmed hat pulled down over his eyes and very long black hair that he hadn't bothered to cut. He spoke with a pronounced foreign accent, and I thought he must be of Greek origin.

"Yes," he said, "I'm not from here."

He was a Cynic, of the school of Diogenes, who called himself a citizen of the world and kept on the move, living from day to day.

"I've heard," he said, "that a man hereabouts rose from the grave. What's true in the tale?"

The news could not possibly have spread like that, so I suspected he was an informer sent by the Romans to trail me.

"That's what they say," I replied.

"Do you believe it?"

I avoided this by saying, "Each one of us rises again. Life is nothing but a succession of men, each derived from

€148

another. One dies, and another takes his place. That is resurrection, I feel—continuity. What does your school think of this?"

"My school rejects everything, even thought. Thought doesn't exist, all that exists is man, who wanders in space among the atoms. And anyone who bothers to create systems is a fool. But who was this fellow?"

I told him what had happened but attributed my own idea, that of the change of appearances, to someone else, whom I called unbalanced.

"It's the result of doing too many miracles," I remarked cautiously, "which means you finally make people believe the impossible."

"But the capacity to do miracles," said the man, walking fast, head down, "has no bounds, if you have it."

I stopped to look at him. "Then you do believe in the capacity to do miracles?"

We had reached a country inn, exposed to the sun, with a few tufts of tamarisk around it, and he said: "Let's eat. You pay."

He explained that this was the rule of his school: to refuse this world's goods and expect whoever had them to give them to you. In that heat, we were the only travellers, and as we sat eating in a dark corner he said: "It's not a matter of knowing how to do miracles. It's a matter of wanting them to happen."

"Who's supposed to want them?" I asked. "The man who performs them, or the man who undergoes them?"

"The man who undergoes them, of course."

"All right, then. I want you to do a miracle!" I exclaimed, clearly meaning it as a joke.

"But you're asking without enough will."

"But if someone were to ask you, really meaning it, could you do one?"

His eyes glittered in the darkness. "Why not?"

He shouted, "More wine! Asking's the trouble."

He shouted, "Bread!"

He dipped it in the wine and ate with enjoyment.

"Sometimes," he went on, "I feel sorry to see people giving and thinking they're doing something virtuous. The truth is, giving's easy, because it's a passive act. What's hard is asking. Asking is a conquest. It is life."

"In other words," I said, "life belongs to the man who can take it."

"Yes, that's true," he said, dipping in his bread. "Never give, always take. Personal sacrifice is nonsense. And we Cynics have understood this better than the rest. Simple understanding of man. Do you see?"

He swung his head in a way that made his eyes under the hat brim look like lanterns, appearing and disappearing. "And where did the fellow who rose end up?"

"That's what we'd all like to know," I replied.

"Has he been seen?"

"Yes. I saw him myself."

"Did you actually touch him?"

"Yes."

"Yet you doubt that he's real."

I was silent. The cicadas were drunk, and the innkeeper's wife, who had stayed to keep an eye on us behind the marble counter, was nodding with sleepiness. In the heat we were the only two people awake.

"Maybe," the stranger went on sharply, "this idea of changed appearances isn't wrong after all. Maybe the man never died and is now in hiding. But if another man died in his place, where would his body have gone to? Maybe stolen and hidden. It makes sense. But everything makes sense in this world, which is why we Cynics don't believe in any truth."

He had raised his arms and uncovered his wrists, as if to cool himself, then, spreading his hands out on the table, he stayed still in that position.

There were holes in his wrists. I leaned over to examine them.

"How did you get these?" I asked, in such an acute state of tension that I was afraid I couldn't bear it.

"These? Smallpox."

"They never healed," I remarked, hating him.

He shrugged, without answering.

"Have you any others?"

He nodded, indifferently. "I must go now. Thanks for the meal."

"Wait! I'm coming with you!"

He stood still in the white road, wrapped around in his dark clothes, his sweat-soaked hair hanging from his temples like string. Now that I could, I looked at his feet. He was wearing shoes that covered them. I could not resist asking.

"Forgive me, but I'm a doctor and your case interests me. Did the smallpox leave any scars on your feet as well?"

He came close to me, threateningly: "It's the custom of my school to be silent after meals, to meditate on digestion, the fount of life."

So we reached Emmaus in silence. He walked so fast that I could hardly keep up, and every now and then I had to run to do so. At the first houses he stopped.

"I'll lodge at the inn in the square. You pay."

I followed him, worn out and obedient; took lodgings and left him, wishing him goodnight. But next morning he had vanished. They told me he had left at dawn, going north.

I saw my rich patient and lost no time in taking the same road.

* * *

I soon reached Galilee, with a lift on a cart, and stopped at Capharnaum. "You?" Peter greeted me, cautiously opening his front door slightly. With relief he asked me in and we exchanged news. He told me, though disappointedly, that he had gone back to normal life, thus placating his wife whom he had neglected lately and who in fact had greeted me rather coolly.

After supper, sitting under the olive trees among pots of geraniums, he confessed to me with pain: "I've started doubting myself, you know. The corpse's disappearance doesn't necessarily mean he rose again. Maybe we just saw a ghost that deluded us it was flesh, while the Temple people stole his body, or the Romans took it to test our resistance."

He took his head between his hands.

John, Thaddeus, Andrew and the others came along, and we sat silently in the soft evening air, as if we wanted to communicate our inexpressible thoughts without speaking. When it was fully night Peter rose to go to work and the others followed him.

"Come too, if you like," he suggested. Afterwards he added, while the others were loading their nets into the boat: "I've a guilty conscience for treating you so badly at Luke's."

"I'm so happy," I said, cheating him over the real object of my visit, "to be here with you."

They had chosen a part of the lake where there were reeds near the bank, and tench were plentiful at that time of year. I sat in the prow, while the others rowed. About midnight they first cast their nets. I looked at the moon, swaying above the calm sea, and the hills were light as day. Occasionally a fish leaped up, making rings in the water. I thought of my years of study and experimental research, and my fascination with exact science, and then of my feeling of its insufficiency, my restlessness, and wondered what destiny had brought me to that point, which was concerned with neither medicine nor fishing.

We caught a hundredweight of fish and when we went back to the shore at dawn we were tired but tranquil. Work gave us a feeling of certainty, at least. When we had spread out the nets to dry and prepared the baskets for market, we were resting on the still empty shore with the moon behind us, only now beginning to turn pale; and a figure I recognized at once came towards us. With my heart thudding, I hid behind the boat.

"Good catch?" the stranger greeted us. Peter hardly looked at him, and said yes. As he waited there, Peter realized what he wanted, and he rose and gave him two tench to eat himself or to sell.

The man in the wide-brimmed hat had crouched down someway off and was neatly lighting a small fire, on which he laid the two fish. He roasted them with the movements of a man used to living with whatever is handy, who enjoys doing without what is superfluous. Peter's wife was serving us a meal at the same time, and handed the stranger bread and a cup, with a slightly suspicious glance. The man meantime asked about what we were doing, whether fishing paid well, and if they needed anyone to work for them.

"Now that's something we can always use," Peter said, chewing. "The fishing's good."

"Maybe I could stay a few weeks."

"Stay then," said Peter. "It's ten shekels a day, plus your keep."

"Do you really mean it?"

"Why yes," said Peter.

"Really and truly?"

Peter answered: "Yes."

Then, with no need for it, the man began taking off his shoes and rolling up the sleeves of his tunic, and then he stood before us. No one looked at him, as everyone was bent over the food. But when Peter looked up his hand shook so much that the cup fell from it.

"Is it he?" he exclaimed breathlessly. The others were grouped around him, unbelievingly.

"Who?" said Andrew.

"Is it he?" Peter repeated with tears in his eyes. Then he said: "No, it's impossible."

"It is, it is!" cried John.

Peter's wife, who came out of the house at that moment, recognized him at once and shouted furiously: "Is that lazy lout from Nazareth back again?"

Peter covered her mouth. Then he said to the stranger, almost aggressively:

€154

"What does all this mean?"

"You can just get out, this minute!" his wife yelled, freeing herself. "Get out, get away!"

Peter fell on his knees, and repeated in a trembling voice: "What does it mean?"

"Peace be with you," the man said, no longer speaking with a foreign accent. He had taken off his hat, his hair and his false beard and was looking at us. Except for me, lying hidden, they all shielded their dazzled eyes, while the sun rose behind Jesus. John crawled over to Jesus and laid his lips on the wounds of his feet. And one by one the others did too. Peter's wife had fainted.

"Can't you see he's tricking you!" I cried, coming out. They glared at me, their eyes like burning coals.

"You dog!" Peter cried.

"He never died!" I said. "And now he's hiding from the police!"

I flung myself forward, shouting straight at him: "Where have you hidden Simon's body?"

All my comrades leaped on me, kicking and punching, and dragging me to the water. I managed to get away from them and hide in the wood, but they caught up with me and whipped my face with bracken, and even bit me. I held out, though. And when I heard Thaddeus shouting: "Let's crucify the swine!" I opened my arms and stood in that position on the torn-up bracken. Panting and furious, they looked at me, and again Peter took his head in his hands, biting his fingers with sorrow.

"Oh, Thomas, Thomas," he wept on my breast, "why won't you believe?"

The others kept beating their heads as well, and now

they kissed my hands and tried to lead me back to Jesus, who stood waiting. When I was before him, my face bleeding, I said: "No, I still don't believe. Another man suffered in your place, as I am suffering at this moment."

He gave no answer, but having put on his shoes and turned down his sleeves turned to the lake, and we watched him walking on its surface towards the sun, and vanishing from sight.

"Murderer!" I shouted after him, walking into the water. "Murderer!"

And now I was weeping too.

*　*　*

I have written this account in order to give it to Peter when people can think more calmly and historical truth can be looked at objectively. At present, I merely doubt, I do not dismiss possibilities. Simon of Cyrene was never found again. Was it really he who was crucified? Does the figure of Jesus have no meaning? And if there was no basis for my incredulity and it was really Jesus who suffered martyrdom, then should I not be punished? But in any case, what difference does it make . . . A man suffered on the cross. Is it so important to know who he was?